A CHANGE OF HEART

A Change Of Heart

by

Louise Armstrong

Dales Large Print Books
Long Preston, North Yorkshire,
BD23 4ND, England.

British Library Cataloguing in Publication Data.

Armstrong, Louise
    A change of heart.

       A catalogue record of this book is
       available from the British Library

       ISBN   978-1-84262-612-2 pbk

First published in Great Britain in 2007
by D.C. Thomson & Co. Ltd.

Copyright © Louise Armstrong 2007

Cover illustration © Nigel Chamberlain by arrangement with
Alison Eldred

The moral right of the author has been asserted

Published in Large Print 2008 by arrangement with
Louise Armstrong

Dales Large Print is an imprint of Library Magna Books Ltd.

Printed and bound in Great Britain by
T.J. (International) Ltd., Cornwall, PL28 8RW

1

A Difficult Decision

Nikki Marlow's fingers drummed faster and faster on the polished mahogany boardroom table. She was trying very hard to keep her cool and to behave in a professional manner but because she was feeling so tired and ill it was hard for her to hide her exasperation.

So, when she opened her mouth to speak the words snapped out more sharply than she'd intended. 'You're wasting my time,' she told the man sitting across the table from her.

Alexander Davidson squared his massive shoulders and gave her a long, thoroughly measuring look.

His knitted cable sweater and comfortable corduroy trousers made him look like a geography teacher about to set off on a field trip but Nikki couldn't help noticing that his homely jersey was filled out by a well-muscled chest, and that he had gorgeous black hair.

Nikki's awareness of his obvious attractions did nothing to calm her jangled nerves. She struggled to control her reaction to him and to keep her voice as normal as possible.

'We must cancel the order from the Middle East,' she insisted.

Alexander studied her carefully before he answered, speaking softly.

'Cancel an order for five thousand top-of-the-range Windsor prams? Absolutely not. We start production tomorrow.'

Nikki couldn't believe what she was hearing.

'Are you crazy? This factory closes tonight. And don't try to tell me that this order could save the business. You'll lose money on this order, not make it!'

Nikki flipped back her blonde hair and swept an impatient glance around the boardroom. None of the faces were friendly and she wondered if she had any supporters at all.

At the head of the table, Norman Thompson, a white-haired, rather plump man, was trembling with anger.

'I've never heard the like in all my born days. I've managed this factory for the best part of thirty years! Thirty years, I tell you! And now this snip of a girl wants to close us down! Who does she think she is?'

At the head of the boardroom table Lord Foulridge cleared his throat, took off his glasses, and polished them carefully before he spoke.

'Miss Marlow has been appointed as Official Receiver and was chosen because her firm has great experience dealing with companies in the same situation as that in which Davidson's Baby Carriage Company finds itself.'

A red-haired man in well-worn overalls snorted.

'Broke, you mean! I'm not afraid to call a spade bankrupt, your lordship.'

Lord Foulridge raised his eyebrows.

'Do please call me Hugh. And yes, one must admit that the prospects for the company look bleak. But this might be a good time for me to say to Miss Marlow that, although I am here to represent the interests of the bank, the board members are unanimous in asking you to make every effort to construct a rescue package.'

Nikki honestly couldn't understand his point of view.

'You'll be lucky to see any of your investment back as it is. Why throw good money after bad?'

Lord Foulridge smiled so serenely that

you would never have guessed he was discussing the prospect of losing six million pounds of his bank's money.

'Jobs are tremendously important in this area, and one doesn't like to see a fine old English company go down. Why, I had a Davidson's Baby Carriage myself; a Chatsworth, I think the model was.'

A nostalgic smile lit the face of Olivia Marsden, who had been sent to the meeting by the insurance company connected with the factory.

She touched her silver-grey coiffure as she spoke in her very deep voice.

'Mine was a Kensington. I can still remember Nanny wheeling me around the park.'

She and Lord Foulridge turned to smile at each other.

Nikki felt frustrated and not in control. She longed for the bustle and glowing computer screens of her office at Bosworth's Chartered Accountants.

She wasn't comfortable with the atmosphere in this room. The very air was alien to her. It was cold and damp and smelt of the moor outside. Nikki rarely left central Manchester. The landscape of industrial Yorkshire chilled her. She could still hardly believe that her car was parked in a cobbled yard beneath a set of coal-black chimneys. It was so old-fashioned.

The people didn't feel real to her, either.

Lord Foulridge and Olivia Marsden exuded an air of tweedy confidence that seemed a world away from anything to do with bankruptcy.

The young, red-haired engineer was hard to read because of his thick black-rimmed glasses, but he seemed to have a good grasp of the situation that the company was in, and he looked intelligent.

Which was more than could be said about the bad-tempered man who claimed to have been managing the company for thirty years. If that were the case, then it was probably his fault that the pram company was in such difficulties.

And as for Alexander Davidson, there had been nothing in her original briefing about him. He was the owner's nephew and had turned up unexpectedly at the meeting brandishing power of attorney.

Nikki watched him out of the corner of her eye and decided that she'd need to be wary of him. He might seem slow and a bit of a plodder but there was steel in him and he'd been opposing her from the minute they'd sat down at the table.

He'd seemed to be studying the gilt-framed oil portraits of long-gone Davidson family members that hung around the room, but now – as if he felt Nikki's attention on him – he lifted his long-lashed gaze and turned it directly on her.

His eyes were brown and very steady as they met her grey ones. For some reason, the expression on his face made Nikki feel nervous.

Lord Foulridge and Olivia Marsden were still discussing their childhood prams and comparing nannies.

Nikki cleared her throat and once again her voice came out more harshly than she had intended.

'Do you think we could continue?' she demanded.

'My goodness, yes,' apologised Hugh Foulridge, taking a look at his gold watch. 'Oh! It's nearly ten o'clock. Do we all agree that we're in a position to close for the evening.'

'No!' exploded Nikki. She glared at Alexander. 'Mr Davidson still wants the factory to start work on the Middle Eastern order in the morning. That order will lose money, and I won't have it.'

Alexander stared hard at Nikki before turning to look at Olivia and Hugh. A message seemed to pass between the three of them and Nikki didn't like that at all. It was as if they understood something that she didn't.

Lord Foulridge leant forward and spoke to her gently.

'We understand your point of view, Nikki, but I'm sure you're aware that there may be more than one way of looking at the situation.'

She could feel herself smouldering. 'This factory is bankrupt. What other view can there be?'

It was Alexander who answered her. She saw a hot spark of anger deep in his eyes, but his slow way of talking didn't change at all.

'It doesn't make sense to close down the factory at this time. If you'll come to my office tomorrow, I'll go over the figures with you.'

'Why not now?'

He gave a short laugh. 'You might be superhuman, but I'm not. I've been here since six o'clock this morning.'

She tried to provoke him. 'I've been on the go since five.'

His unruffled smile ignored the challenge. 'Well, I'm sorry but I've had enough for one day,' he told her.

Nikki tried to meet his eyes and couldn't.

Her cheeks felt hot and her gaze fell to the table. She knew instinctively that she would never shift him, but she was not going to back down.

'There is absolutely no point in discussing this further. You must cancel the Middle Eastern order,' she snapped at him.

He regarded her with distaste, but as ever his response came slowly and courteously. 'But you haven't seen my figures yet.'

'If you weren't so slow in coming to the point, I could have looked at fifty sets of figures and we could all have been home an hour ago!'

At last she heard an edge to his voice. 'Are you certain you fully understand the situation?' he asked her.

Nikki was furious. 'Do you think I'm stupid?'

'No, but you're so hasty that you make me nervous. You've only been in this factory for a few hours. Are you sure you've grasped the whole picture?'

Nikki suddenly wondered if Alexander could be right. A few hours to understand how a highly specialised business worked? She looked uncertainly at Lord Foulridge who smiled at her benignly, and at Olivia Marsden who was smiling at Alexander.

Nikki felt unusually defensive.

'I'm used to making quick decisions,' she said.

Olivia's kind blue eyes rested on Nikki. 'It would be wise of you to recognise the special circumstances that apply to this company, my dear. Alexander has a factory of his own and has a lot of manufacturing experience. Why don't you two get together before our next meeting and discuss the matter further? Our next meeting's on Wednesday, isn't it, Hugh?'

Lord Foulridge pulled out a leather personal organiser and peered at it over the top of his gold-rimmed spectacles.

'Absolutely. The day after tomorrow. Is that agreeable to everyone?'

There was a murmur of consent from around the table and then the elderly manager flounced out and the engineer in the dark overalls walked after him, a bleak expression on his white, tired face.

The engineer alone seems to understand that there's no hope, thought Nikki.

Meanwhile, Alexander was ushering Hugh and Olivia out of the boardroom and along the corridor towards the exit.

Nikki was furious – with herself for being so snappy and discourteous and with Alexander Davidson for not only having better manners but for not being prepared to unquestioningly carry out her instructions.

From what she had been able to gather, he had only been at the factory for a week himself. How much of an expert did that make him?

Nikki walked outside to the factory yard and shivered in the cold northern air. She wrapped her arms around herself as if for protection. Everyone else had driven away home and she and Alexander were now alone together. She sneaked a glance at him from under her lashes, and with a jolt of her heart realised that he was looking straight back at her.

She didn't stop to think before she snapped at him, 'What are you looking at me like that for? You've got your way – but only for now. I'm willing to meet you tomorrow but what can you possibly say to persuade me to keep the factory open?'

Nikki shivered and shifted from foot to foot as she waited for his response. Her kitten-heeled shoes scraped on the cobbles that made up the factory yard. She was cold, she had a pain in her chest, and she was tired of waiting.

'Well?'

Alexander finally spoke, in an unruffled voice.

'I've been wondering all evening why it is that you're so tense.'

Startled, her gaze few up to meet his. His dark brown eyes were examining her as if he wanted to see into her very soul. The intimacy of his look alarmed her.

'Don't let's get personal. The only reason I'm talking to you at all is because I want to save as much as I can from the wreckage.'

The last thing she expected was a snort of laughter.

'I hardly think you've come galloping up north like the Lone Ranger to save the day, have you?'

Nikki spoke through gritted teeth. 'I'll just remind you that I'm a fully qualified chartered accountant and that I'm here in my capacity as Official Receiver.'

There followed another of the long pauses that he seemed to specialise in and she wondered if she was ever going to get a response from him.

She was just about to turn and walk away when she saw his shoulders shift slightly and he finally answered her.

'Businesses are made up of people. People

are personal.'

She felt a kind of baffled fury. It had been so long since she'd yelled at him that she couldn't remember if he was answering a legitimate question or not. She was glad when a middle-aged security man in uniform approached them.

'You'll be OK to lock up now, Dave. We're going home,' said Alexander. 'The boardroom meeting is finished.'

'Very good, sir. Shall I walk you to your car, Miss Marlow?'

'No, thank you. There's no need,' she said, walking away.

Nikki's bright red sports car was parked farther away than Alexander's long, low Jaguar, but she was inside and belted up before he'd even opened the door of his own car.

She snapped on the stereo, revved the engine and reversed, ready to pull out of the car park.

Alexander – she saw with disbelief – seemed to be leaning against his car staring up at the sky.

'Watching the stars!' she said to herself in amazement. 'His factory is about to be closed down, and he's standing around, watching the stars!'

And although she knew it was childish, she zoomed out of the factory entrance with a screech of wheels and a satisfying spray of gravel.

2

A Golden Goose

When Nikki arrived at the factory at half-past seven the next morning, there was a note on her desk that read, *See you in my office at 9.30 a.m. Staff meeting in the canteen at 11.00 a.m. A.D.*

She crumpled the scrap of paper in her hand before flinging it to the floor. The scrunched-up ball promptly vanished into the chaos lying around her; the room she'd been given to work in was full of junk: bolts of material, boxes of screws, cans of oil, yellowing invoices, broken machinery parts, all of it well stirred and covered in cobwebs and dust. However, she knew that there wasn't a better room because she'd checked, the evening before.

'No wonder they've gone broke,' she

grumbled, crawling over the ancient carpet and plugging her laptop into a dangerously old-fashioned looking socket.

She stood up and brushed at some grubby marks on her white shirt.

'For goodness' sake,' she muttered.

Her mood wasn't improved by the fact that she couldn't get through to her secretary back at her office at Bosworth's until almost nine o'clock.

'Marie! Where have you been?' she snapped, when at long last her call was answered.

'Oh, I'm so sorry, Nikki, but I was staying at Michael's last night and it's a nightmare journey to get to work from his place.'

'Marie, I don't know why you bother with him. He walks all over you. You keep saying that you want to get married and settle down but you'll never have that with him. You should dump him and find yourself a nice bloke.'

'But he's so much fun, Nikki. And I know he loves me, really.' Her assistant's tone was injured.

Pain clawed at Nikki's heart. How often had her mother said those very words, trying to excuse some bad behaviour on the part of her latest toyboy? And the men her mother married always let her down.

Nikki wanted to make Marie understand that it was no good ignoring the warning signals. That was how women's hearts got broken.

'You're a wonderful person, Marie. You deserve better,' she insisted.

A long sigh greeted her pep talk.

'It's so unfair, Nikki. There's you – you who could have any man you want, but you aren't interested and don't want to get married; and here's me, who does,' complained Marie. 'But one day you'll meet someone special like Michael, then you'll understand.'

Nikki wished she could reach down the phone and shake her assistant. Marie was a sweet girl and couldn't see that Michael was using her.

Nikki also suspected that Michael was using Marie to gain information about some of Bosworth's clients. They had several famous names on their books and Nikki had several times warned Marie about confidentiality, but she was afraid that her secretary was passing on titbits of information to Michael who then sold them on to the newspapers.

Marie needed an honest man, someone who was kind and who loved her for herself, someone a bit slower and less flashy. Someone who said less and meant more.

To Nikki's horror, her mind suddenly threw up a picture of Alexander Davidson. Where had that come from?

'We'd better get on with some work, Marie,' she said, pushing her thoughts to one side.

Nikki looked through the 'To Do' list that she'd written last night and asked Marie several questions relating to the work that Nikki had left for her while she was away.

Marie's responses were frustrating, and Nikki despaired of the way she had to push her secretary to get on with things all the time. Nikki hardly dared ask her about the figures she'd been putting together for a famous rock star. However, Marie sounded proud when she answered.

'You don't need to worry about that. Allen Green is looking after it.'

Nikki couldn't control her response.

'Allen–! How could you be so silly, Marie? Allen Green's been trying for months to take that account from me. I can't believe you gave him information about my client! How could you betray me like this?'

A hard lump rose up in Nikki's chest and throttled the rest of her angry words. She sat holding the phone, breathing very fast, wondering what kind of woman she was turning into. Her stomach and chest hurt all the time these days, but that was no excuse for her temper. She would apologise as soon as she could get a word in.

'Mr Bosworth himself told me to give Allen the information,' Marie was saying. 'There's no way I can do it all, Nikki, not even for a week. I just can't carry the work-load that you do. And I'm only a secretary. You can't expect me to make decisions the way you do, not when they involve millions of pounds.'

'It's only numbers,' said Nikki wearily. 'They don't mean anything.'

After a long silence, Marie said in a small voice, 'I'm sorry.'

'No, Marie, *I'm* sorry. Don't worry – I'll fight Allen for my rock star when I get back.'

'How long will you be away from the office?'

'Not long. There's no chance of a recovery package here.'

'Well,' said Marie, 'I hope you'll be back in time for Brenda's party. At the last one–'

'Spare me the gossip, Marie, I'll ring you again later,' Nikki told her.

Nikki put down the phone feeling annoyed that her secretary couldn't show more initiative. You couldn't rely on anyone else to get things right, that was for sure.

Her laptop alarm chimed softly, prompting her to look at her watch. It was time for her first meeting of the day.

She walked quickly to the office at the opposite end of the corridor. A hand-printed card on the door announced that Alexander Davidson was to be found inside. Nikki rapped hard.

As she waited, she was aware of the vibrations of working machinery – a distant hum that had been there all morning, she realised, just below the threshold of awareness.

She hadn't been around the manufacturing side of the factory yet. She would go and look at it as soon as this interview was over.

She knocked on the door again. It would be so like this big, slow man to take half an hour to get up from his desk and come to the door!

Then Nikki heard a movement inside the office and decided that he was deliberately keeping her waiting. Well, she wasn't having that!

She pushed the door open and stalked in.

Sunlight poured in through office windows

that had been polished until they sparkled, allowing golden beams to light up the man who was standing in the centre of the room, his back to her, looking like a Greek statue in a spotlight. He held a towel in one hand and was shirtless, his back tanned and muscular.

Nikki took a step backwards and her hands flew to her mouth as 'Oh!' escaped involuntarily.

Alexander Davidson, rubbing at his coal-black hair with the towel, turned slowly to look at her from under wet eyelashes. He smiled at her, then he turned to pick up the fleece sweater that lay on his desk, pulling it on over his bare chest.

'I went for a run and then used the factory shower,' he said in explanation.

'Well, it's made you late for our meeting,' she replied sharply.

Alexander rolled up his towel, put it away in a sports bag, and then looked at the clock on the wall. It said nine-thirty precisely. He turned to stare at her. His expression contained a mixture of surprise and contempt.

Eventually he said slowly, 'I'm sorry if you feel that I kept you waiting. I'll make us some coffee.'

'I don't have time for coffee.'

'Well, maybe you don't, but I do. Hold on

until I put away my running kit and I'll switch on the machine.'

Nikki bit back a retort and stamped over to the coffee machine. They'd be another half an hour if she waited for him to make it. She spooned coffee into the gleaming new machine and filled it with water before snapping on the switch.

She clattered the cups and spoons. 'How do you like your coffee?'

'Black.'

A few minutes later she banged two cups of coffee on to his desk and pulled up the only empty chair. Black streaks appeared on the skirt of her new beige suit. Whoever had cleaned his office had made a lovely job of the windows but had missed the chair.

Nikki's temper flared.

'Suppose you explain to me why you want to start work on an order that will lose the factory money?'

She heard the venom in her voice and added more reasonably, 'I promise I'll try to understand.'

Alexander gave her a wry look, and with maddening calm reached for a pad of lined A4 paper. He tapped on the pad with his pencil.

'How much do you know about manufacturing, Nikki?'

She met the expression in his eyes and felt surprise. There was warmth, intimacy, even liking in his deep brown gaze. She felt herself thawing slightly. Was he about to see reason? She took a sip of her coffee. It was aromatic and smooth. She smiled.

'What do I know about manufacturing? Making a profit. That's what I know, and that's all that matters.'

The warmth died in Alexander's eyes and she felt as if a cloud had passed over the sun.

'That might be the name of your game, Nikki, but what about the long-term health of the company? Do you want to kill the goose that lays the golden egg?'

She regretted her soft moment. She put her cup back on the desk.

He stared at her for a long moment, waiting for her answer.

'So, what about the long-term health of the goose?' he prompted.

Nikki didn't like his superior manner.

'Are you fantasising about making this factory profitable? Well, let me just remind you that I'm sitting here because this precious factory owes close to six million pounds!'

'If you kill the goose there'll never be any

more golden eggs.'

'Will you stop blathering on about geese?'

Alexander's long slow gaze didn't blink.

'I deal in actual factories,' he told her. 'You deal in numbers on a computer screen. Which of us is more likely to understand the realities of manufacturing?'

'Just tell me what you're getting at,' said Nikki, sighing. But inside she acknowledged his barb. Yes, she handled millions of pounds for her clients but she had never set foot in a factory before and never would again!

She wished he would get to the point. She felt uncomfortable in the silence. It left too much time to think.

'Start talking!' she growled at him.

'I'm trying to decide how to make this simple.'

Nikki fumed into the silence that followed. Her gaze followed the progress of his pen as it moved deliberately over the page, making two neat columns of figures. He had big, strong hands, she noticed. Strong like the rest of him. He might be slow but she acknowledged that he was tough mentally, forbiddingly tough, under his laid-back exterior.

He also seemed very confident that he was going to convince her that it made sound economic sense to take on work that would lose the factory money.

Half an hour later she was staring at his face in total disbelief.

'So, what you're saying is that if we don't make those prams – losing a quarter of a million pounds on the order – then we'll lose half a million pounds instead, because it's going to take at least three months to sell up and during that time the factory will be standing idle?'

He nodded. 'Better to lose a quarter of a million than a half.'

Nikki pulled the pad of figures towards her and ran over them again, tapping each figure with a pencil as she went. He couldn't be right!

She tasted cold bitterness in her mouth and realised she'd chewed right through the pencil to the lead. She flung it on to the desk and reached for her calculator, but the figures still came out the same. Even if they saved on wages by sacking all the staff today, there was still rent, rates, ground rent, utilities, loan interest … money for nothing if the factory wasn't working. And it would take a month at least to carry out the inventory, and then probably another month to sell off the stock and machines. That took them slap-bang up to the nuisance of the Christmas holidays.

Nikki chewed her lip as she realised that she was going to be tied to working at Davidson's Baby Carriage Company until at least the New Year.

She was used to juggling figures, pulling information down off a screen. She hadn't realised how long it would take to carry out an inventory or that you couldn't just magically transport a machine from one end of England to the other. Real equipment had to be counted, measured, valued, advertised, sold, unscrewed, packed, transported. It all took time.

Her quick brain raced through the equation and came to an unwelcome conclusion: Alexander was right.

Finally, she had no choice but to lift her head and meet his eyes.

'OK. We'll do it your way.'

There was no triumph in his gaze. He just spoke in his slow manner.

'And this way we keep the machinery ticking over,' he told her. 'The prams are out in the world, advertising the company; we might become fashionable again. Who knows, a neighbouring oil state might decide they want fifty thousand prams, and we *would* make a profit on that order. Then the factory won't have to close.'

Nikki gazed at him. 'You're such an optimist,' she said, speaking nearly as slowly as he did.

He gave her a smile. 'People will always fall in love and have babies, and babies need prams.'

Nikki's temper flared before she could ask herself why his words had made her so angry.

'You're talking like this order is a good thing, but it's crazy to lose money just to keep a factory running. I can't understand why Hugh and Olivia want to keep going.'

'Maybe they're a little more long-sighted than you.'

Nikki jumped to her feet. Debt terrified her. This was her first appointment as Official Receiver, and Alexander had persuaded her to sanction a course of action that was going to cost a quarter of a million pounds over the next month, and possibly the next as well. An extra half a million pounds of debt.

How would she explain that to her employers if things went wrong?

'It's only common sense to minimise the losses,' she said. 'But long term, this factory must close as soon as possible.'

'Money isn't the only motive to take into consideration.'

'Money means everything.'

From the moment she'd chosen accountancy as a career, Nikki had had the standard lecture many times. People would look saintly and tell her she was a money-grubber and that money was the root of all evil. But Nikki knew her Bible better than they did.

She waited for her opportunity to tell Alexander that it was actually the love of money that was the root of all evil.

Then the pains that never quite went away in her chest and stomach stepped up and began hurting a lot.

She wished she could go home and lie on the sofa with Buffy, her golden Labrador.

'I'm going to fax Hugh and Olivia,' she announced, annoyed to find that her voice wasn't quite steady. 'I'm going to tell them they're going to have to demolish this factory – if not now then in the very near future – and then I'm going back to Manchester – the real world.'

She marched out of the door and slammed it behind her as hard as she could. The flimsy partition walls rattled in their sockets and a mess of cobwebs dropped from the ceiling.

Shuddering, Nikki brushed at the sticky

dust that landed on her shoulder. She'd never imagined her first job out in the field would be so difficult, but if she wanted to be offered a partnership at Bosworth's she was going to have to make a clean job of this insolvency case.

She knew that the senior partners in her firm viewed her with approval, but she also knew how quickly she could lose that approval. Only the best were invited to join the inner circle. And to be the best she was going to have to get on top of the situation at the Davidson Baby Carriage Company.

Nikki marched around the factory clutching her notebook, ignoring the wonderful assortment of grubby smears and black marks that collected on her clothes as she hurried around taking an overview, making notes. The working parts of the factory were in no better shape than the offices.

Demolition really was the only answer, as soon as the inventory was complete and they'd sold what they could.

As eleven o'clock approached, Nikki glanced at her watch and headed for the factory meeting.

The white-haired manager was standing on a chair at the front of the canteen. His chest was puffed out like a rooster about to crow and Nikki couldn't help smiling a little. He clearly loved an audience. The factory workers were grouped around him.

'Attention, everybody!' the manager shouted, clapping his hands together.

Nikki watched the stir that ran around the room, noticing the folded arms and hostile expressions. Few of the workers were looking directly at the man's face. It didn't look as if he was very popular with them.

Then a door opened at the back of the canteen, and Alexander Davidson strolled towards the front of the room, coming to a halt next to Nikki.

He raised one eyebrow. 'I thought you'd gone back to Manchester?'

To her annoyance, she blushed.

'I'll leave when things are in good order, not before,' she told him crisply.

The elderly manager clapped his hands again.

'Now then, you all know me – Norman Thompson, senior manager for many a year,' he began to address the workers. 'I know you're all worried about the company, but I want you to know that everything's all right and that I'm in charge while Albert Davidson, the owner, is away. I've just rung the nursing home and the Matron herself assures me that Albert's resting very comfortably, very comfortably indeed. He'll be back at work before we know it. In the meantime, we're lucky to have his nephew, Alexander Davidson, to give us a hand.'

There was a belligerent mutter from the back of the room.

'Who's he when he's at home?'

'What? You've never heard of Smart Fabric and the man who made millions from it? His factory's a showcase. It won an award.'

Nikki saw the employees respond to this. They looked with interest at Alexander, and then back at the manager, willing now to hear more.

Norman Thompson stuck out his chest boastfully.

'That's right, he knows what he's doing does Alexander, and so do I! We've got plans for this factory, we have. It's all worked out. Trust me. We've got some fantastic new orders and we'll be back in full production in no time.'

Nikki was stunned by his bravado. He certainly didn't sound like a man who'd been to an insolvency meeting only the night before. And as he continued, it became plain that he wasn't going to admit that the receiver was on the premises.

She bit her lip, registering that people were a lot more difficult to control than figures in a book. The workers, however, looked happier. They seemed to have believed Norman's lying report.

A man who wore a badge that said 'chargehand' stepped forward out of the crowd.

'Mr Thompson, when can we have the details of the new orders?'

'Soon, and you'll be bowled over by them,' Norman Thompson boasted. 'The factory will soon be back on its feet.'

Before the man could ask any more questions, Norman jumped down from his chair and ran over to Nikki. He dragged over a wooden bench, jumped up and pulled Nikki up beside him, displaying her to the workers.

'And this charming young lady is going to help us!' he announced.

Wolf whistles rent the air. Nikki could have throttled the old twister. She hated the feeling that everyone was looking at her. What a great first impression she must be making! There were cobwebs in her blonde hair, her suit was a mess, and her high-heeled shoes teetered on the wooden surface of the bench.

She was glad when Alexander moved up beside her and offered her his arm. She'd have liked to get down off the bench by herself, but it was a long way to the ground and she felt her feet go from beneath her. Rather than sprawl on the floor, she hurled herself at Alexander. He caught her easily and steadied her until she had her balance.

'Thank you,' she muttered.

Alexander didn't say a word, but she was aware of his masculine strength beside her. His chest muscles had felt like a steel wall, but his soft hair had brushed her cheek as he caught her. She was curiously reluctant to turn away from his warmth.

Norman Thompson was dismissing the staff.

'Back to work,' he called, 'and trust me! I've got everything in hand.'

Nikki watched as the production workers headed back to the factory floor, chatting animatedly as they went. There was hope on the faces of the people around her. She felt a pain in her heart. For the first time she saw them as real people who would suffer when they lost their jobs. And it was going to be even harder to break the truth to them now that they'd been fed false information. She turned away quickly from her troubling thoughts to reality.

The chargehand had remained behind, looking eager.

'When do we start on the new orders?' he asked Norman Thompson.

Norman waved a pink hand and walked away.

'Don't bother me now,' he snapped.

Nikki was astonished by the manager's attitude.

She spoke kindly to the chargehand. 'I need to check the figures. We'll know better what's happening after the board meeting tomorrow.'

But the man's eyes slid past her. He looked, instead, at Alexander, and spoke to him directly.

'I've jigs to change and such. I need to know now.'

Nikki was furious for a moment. But then she had a vision of herself wobbling on that wooden bench and she knew why the chargehand wasn't taking her seriously. She'd been introduced as a charming young lady, not as a woman with a functioning business brain.

Alexander, to do the man justice, was backing her up. She felt his support.

'Miss Marlow will get back to you as soon as possible.'

The chargehand bustled off, looking less

than satisfied, and Nikki looked directly at Alexander. He was deliberately keeping his expression blank, but at the back of his brown eyes, she saw understanding.

Nikki thought of the terrible debt she was about to commit to.

'I won't give the go-ahead for the order until I'm certain,' she said.

Alexander looked so sympathetic that she spoke honestly and openly.

'It's so much money to owe,' she explained.

His voice was gentle. 'Does debt worry you?' he asked.

Nikki looked down at her shoes. 'It would worry *you* if you'd once lost everything.'

'Everything?' Alexander murmured softly.

Nikki was too caught up in her memories to know how much she was revealing. 'Even my bed. Even my teddy bear.'

She didn't see his expression change as if he understood her now.

'How old were you?'

'Five,' Nikki said.

And she pushed aside the vision of the bailiffs locking her out of her home forever while she sobbed on the pavement.

She pulled herself back to reality and girded herself for the work that needed to be done.

'Come on!' she told Alexander briskly. 'We need to talk in my office.'

'Sure,' he agreed nonchalantly.

Nikki didn't want to meet his eyes. Not getting personal was such a sensible rule.

As Nikki opened the door of her room she was struck all over again by the sense of muddle and decay. She had to get her office cleaned up.

'Alexander, who did you get to clean your windows? Alexander?'

She darted to the door and peered down the corridor. He wasn't there!

Hadn't he been behind her when she'd left the canteen?

Half expecting him to appear at any moment, she used the time to pick up the phone and check on Marie. But Marie seemed to have cotton wool in both ears. She hadn't even made a dent in the list that Nikki had left her a few hours before and she was stubbornly refusing more work.

'Oh, I can't manage what I've got to do already! You'll have to ask Allen to do that,' she complained.

Nikki was furious and banged down the phone.

By the time she was back working at Bosworth's all her clients would have been stolen by the other accountants. But she dared not leave the situation here.

She felt hot as she thought of the factory, casually running up losses of a quarter of a million pounds a month – with her permission. And to think she'd longed for her first outside assignment!

Careless of the dusty surface, she put her arms on her desk and her head on her arms and groaned over her dilemma.

Then she heard slow, slow footsteps in the corridor. Alexander Davidson, condescending to show up at last.

'What do you think you're playing at?' she shouted across the room at him. 'Do you think it's funny to keep me waiting?'

He paused in the doorway, his big figure nearly filling the frame, and looked her over carefully.

Nikki felt a disappointed shock in her heart, because there was real disapproval in his brown eyes as he stared at her. She could hear tightly controlled irritation in his voice as he answered her.

'There's no need for you to be so rude all the time, Nikki. We don't have to like each other, but we do have to work together.'

Her eyes stung and she blinked furiously. She felt like a child that had been thoroughly told off. It was a relief when the phone rang but it was a call for Alexander, not for her, and she passed over the phone with bad grace.

He grasped the receiver in his slow way and took time to thank the telephonist and to reassure her that she had done right to interrupt his meeting.

Nikki sprang to her feet and paced the ancient carpet, listening as Alexander spoke to a fabric supplier. From the one-sided conversation she gathered that the new fabric for this season's pram linings, which had been due to arrive tomorrow, could not now be delivered for six months.

Alexander was – predictably – being incredibly patient. Nikki knew that if she had taken the call she would have been screaming abuse by now.

Alexander put down the phone with apparently sincere good wishes to the manufacturer.

Nikki couldn't restrain herself. 'Why didn't you tell them to forget it? You could find another supplier.'

There was an amused glint in his brown eyes.

'What does it matter? I thought you were all for demolishing the factory?' he asked her.

He had such clear, attractive eyes.

'I haven't changed my mind,' she told him. 'But I don't understand how you can be so laid back about your business dealings.'

He looked at her thoughtfully. His slow scrutiny made her feel uncomfortable. Did the man have nothing to do other than stare at her?

'Sit down,' he said eventually. 'And at least try to relax.'

Much to her surprise, she did as he'd suggested.

After another pause, he went on, 'If I try to explain something to you, will you listen to me with an open mind?'

Nikki felt insulted.

'Of course.'

His next silence seemed to last for an hour. Was he deliberately dragging this out to wind her up? The suspicion sharpened her tone.

'Oh, do hurry up,' she snapped.

She sensed anger in him then, and suddenly realised that this man could be a formidable enemy – but he held his annoyance in check and spoke reasonably.

'Give me a minute to get my thoughts in order. I want to explain to you how the factory got into the mess it's in today,' he said, pulling a sheet of paper towards him and drawing a big circle in the middle of it.

'The goose, otherwise known as the factory,' he said with a smile.

Nikki rolled her eyes, but she kept quiet. If she tackled him about his silly childish metaphor she would only have to perch on her uncomfortable chair for an hour, while he thought of a new one.

'The goose,' she agreed, adding, 'which no longer lays any golden eggs.'

She felt Alexander relax slightly as he registered that she was communicating on his wavelength at last.

'Back in the old days,' he said, 'when it was well looked after, it produced a golden egg every day and everyone was happy. But then my uncle got old and a new generation came along and they convinced him that if they ran the machines full tilt and saved money on maintenance, and cut back on producing new designs, and didn't spend anything on customer research, then they could have two golden eggs every day. And for a while it worked and they made lots of money. But eventually the poor goose broke down under the strain. She just couldn't lay any more eggs.'

'Oh, please!' Nikki scoffed. 'Are you trying

to tug my heartstrings for a pile of bricks and mortar?'

He met her stare. 'I'm trying to keep this factory alive,' he said.

'But it makes no sense. Why pile money and effort into trying to keep a broken-down old factory alive? Look at this place! It's filthy, it's out of date. If you want a factory so much, knock it all down and build a new one.'

'I might do that one day, but not until we can afford it. Nikki, you're thinking of profit and profit alone. There are other issues: tradition; providing employment–'

'Sentiment has no place in business!'

'I'm not sentimental. I'm practical. I didn't come here for family reasons alone. I looked carefully at Davidson's Baby Carriage Company before I agreed to help my uncle. I know it could be a great company again. It's a challenge worth taking on. Won't you be on my side?'

Nikki felt strangely reluctant to oppose him, but she couldn't pretend that she couldn't see the dereliction all around her. Nor could she forget the losses that would mount every month while the factory struggled on.

'It doesn't make economic sense to keep

this factory going. Demolition is the only answer.'

Fury flowed out of Alexander and Nikki felt herself shrink away as she met the shocking intensity in his eyes. His control had slipped. His fist hit the table.

'You've made up your mind and you won't listen. All that matters to you is your own professional safety and profit. Not what's right or what's decent or honest, but getting what you want. And you'll use any tactic, too! You act tough and you talk tough and you push like a spoilt child.'

The vehemence of his attack stunned her.

'You're just annoyed because a female is daring to oppose you. You're afraid of strong women.'

The look in his brown eyes withered her soul. 'You're not a strong woman.'

'I am so!'

'Then why are you hiding behind excuses? Corporate recovery is as much a part of your job as insolvency. You could recommend a rescue package, but you're afraid to stand up and stick your neck out.'

Pain twisted Nikki's heart. She had always stood alone. She had never relied on anyone else in her life. Not even her parents. A mother and father had to both be there before a girl could learn to hide behind them.

But she wasn't going to tell Alexander any more of her history today. She simply lifted her gaze to his face and let him see the reproach she was feeling.

'You have no right to attack me personally.'

She was beginning to get used to his long silences. She studied his face, but his expression was a mystery to her.

His voice was calm again by the time he spoke.

'You are absolutely right, and I apologise.'

Not seeming to move quickly, he rose from his chair and padded across the room. Nikki stared at his departing back for a second and then ran to the door calling after him.

'Wait! What time is the board meeting tomorrow? I need to know.'

She might as well have saved her breath. For all his slow gait, his back was a dark shadow in the distant corridor. He was far enough away for her to assume that he hadn't heard her, and he certainly didn't turn around, or answer her, or acknowledge her in any way.

3

A Shoulder To Cry On

Nikki dressed carefully for the emergency board meeting on Wednesday morning. She decided to wear a designer suit, but she dithered for ages over a top and accessories. She wanted to look businesslike enough to keep Olivia Marsden and Hugh Foulridge on her side, but she also wanted to look attractive.

Not that she wanted to impress Alexander Davidson, of course, but there was no need to let herself go just because she was in the provinces, was there?

In the end, she felt that she'd wasted her time, because when Alexander strolled into the boardroom he didn't seem to notice her outfit at all.

'You're late,' she growled.

He rolled his eyes, looked at the grandfather clock, which said two minutes to the hour, and then looked around the empty room in an exaggerated pantomime before slowly lowering himself into his seat.

'They're having a little trouble in dispatch,' he told her. 'What would you say was the most economical way to wrap a pram for shipment?'

Nikki felt her own ignorance. Figures on the screen were so easy.

She had a sudden vision of a conveyor belt full of lumpy, pram-shaped brown paper parcels and brushed aside the ridiculous urge to smile.

'Put the things in individual cardboard boxes,' she suggested.

'Yes, but they might slide around inside the box. We don't want them damaged in transit.'

Nikki wondered if the man drove his girlfriend mad – if he had a girlfriend? He didn't wear a wedding ring, but that didn't mean that he didn't have a wife at home, or a partner. She reminded herself that his personal life was none of her business, and turned her mind back to wrapping prams.

'Use bubble wrap,' she told him.

'Yes, but do you know how much we've been paying for it? I've got my secretary ringing around for a cheaper source right now.'

'Well, you're wasting your time, and hers! When the factory's demolished–'

Alexander lifted one large hand. 'Let's

postpone this discussion until the others are here.'

Nikki could feel herself bubbling with fury, but there was a quality of quiet, forceful command in his voice that cut short her protest.

Then there were sounds in the corridor, and the receptionist ushered in Norman Thompson, followed by Olivia Marsden from the insurance company and Lord Foulridge from the bank.

Alexander smiled pleasantly at the receptionist. 'Thank you, Tracie. Is Alan Marsh around?'

Nikki guessed that Alan Marsh must be the red-haired man in the dark overalls who'd been at the last board meeting. She didn't see why they needed him.

The receptionist nodded. 'He's researching some material on the internet. Shall I tell him you're ready to start?'

Nettled by the adoring way the receptionist was looking at Alexander, Nikki decided to assert her authority. 'Yes, please, and could you bring in some coffee as well?' she ordered.

They didn't have to wait long for Alan Marsh to join them.

There were smears of grease on his thick

glasses and his overalls looked shabbier than ever.

Norman Thompson glared at him and spoke rudely. 'You're late! And I've told you before about wasting time with that internet rubbish.'

The engineer just shrugged and sat down.

Then Nikki heard a familiar voice outside in the corridor and felt her mouth go dry. She'd been wondering all morning which senior manager would be sent from Bosworth's head office to check up on her, and she didn't know whether to be pleased or offended when the beaming face of Rupert Woodehouse appeared in the doorway.

He didn't have the smartest of financial brains, but he went everywhere, he knew everyone, and he always recommended Bosworth's to his contacts. He was worth millions of pounds in new business, but he wasn't the man to spot a situation spiralling out of control.

Her heart beat a little faster. Did they have such faith in her that they felt her work didn't need checking? But then she reined in her excitement. It could be that the sums involved in this case were considered so trivial by Bosworth's standards that nobody would care if the job went wrong. But *she* cared.

Nikki's spine stiffened, and once again she resolved to do the best possible job for her employers.

'What's up, everybody?' said Rupert genially as he took a seat at the boardroom table. 'Everyone's looking very glum. I know it's not a nice thing to happen, having to demolish–'

Nikki felt as if she were at an important crossroads in her life, as she butted in – 'I know that's what my original fax recommended,' she said, 'but I've re-examined the situation thoroughly and Mr Davidson's figures are valid. Therefore I'm now recommending that we begin production on the Middle Eastern order.'

'What? Changing your mind? That won't go down well.'

It was an effort to meet the surprise in Rupert's blue eyes but suddenly she knew what was the right thing to do. If they stopped work on that order, they would lose half a million pounds.

Nikki looked Rupert directly in the eye and spoke steadily.

'To close down the business as profitably as possible is going to take until the New Year. This order will save us money in the meantime.'

Nikki produced Alexander's figures and went over them with Rupert.

To her astonishment he shrugged and accepted her decision casually.

'Right you are, then, just go ahead. Well, I'll shove off now, unless you need me for anything else?'

As Rupert left the room, Nikki was very aware of Alexander's physical presence beside her. But when he spoke, there was no triumph in his voice, only quiet strength.

'So, we have your official sanction to carry on working?'

She felt as if she were taking another big step down a road that she wasn't sure she wanted to travel down but she drew a deep breath and spoke firmly.

'Yes, you do.'

She could sense the release of tension in the room.

Olivia Marsden and Hugh Foulridge both smiled at her.

'My dear, I'm so pleased.'

'I think we can be confident that this is the way forward.'

The man in the overalls cleared his throat and looked at Nikki.

'Can I go ahead with my designs?' he asked.

Norman Thompson banged his chubby

fist on the table and glowered at him.

'I'm the only designer around here. You stay on the shop floor where you belong.'

More conflict! Nikki's head ached and her insides twisted. Although part of her despised her own weakness, she looked to Alexander for clarification.

'Alan is our top engineer,' he explained, 'and he's been developing a revolutionary new undercarriage. It will make the prams much lighter and more manoeuvrable and will transform the range of buggies.'

Nikki couldn't believe what she was hearing.

'Does nobody here speak English? We're going ahead with the new order to save money, but we're closing this factory as soon as is humanly possible. What do you want to mess around with new designs for?'

She stared at the engineer and he stared right back.

'You don't need to worry, Miss Marlow. I'm working on the plans in my own time.'

'I don't understand you people. Why put in any work at all when you know the place will be gone in three months?'

Nikki noted the painful red flush that sprang up under the young engineer's white skin.

'You never know, Miss Marlow. This is a fine old company, and if any efforts of mine could save it...'

Recognising the sincerity of his words, Nikki fell silent. She didn't know what to say.

Beside her Alexander spoke softly. 'We need new concepts more than anything. The future of the company depends on developing a new range of prams and buggies that can hold their own in the open market. We need strong, original branding that will turn us into market leaders. I've already sourced a good firm of design consultants.'

It was as if Norman Thompson was a firework and Alexander had lit the blue touch paper. White hair flying, the old man bounded to his feet. His chest seemed to swell and his cheeks puffed out in rage.

'I don't like your attitude, young Davidson. I don't like it at all! I don't know what makes you think you're smart enough to sound off about a business you know nothing about. You propose to hire a pack of college boys who'll charge two hundred quid an hour to come up with some fluffy designs when all you have to do is ask me! But what do I know about anything, hey? I've only run this firm for thirty years, after all! Don't you bother to ask me.'

Nikki felt dazed by the volcanic emotions that were erupting all around her. She vowed that once she'd finished at Davidson's she'd never leave her office at Bosworth's again.

She knew that she should pull herself together and point out that this whole argument was futile. The Davidson Baby Carriage Company needed no new designs. It wouldn't exist after the New Year.

But it was Alexander who calmed the situation. He smiled benignly at the elderly man, and even more warmly at Alan, the engineer.

'I'm sorry you should feel this way, Norman, but we have to get a fresh viewpoint on the business if we've any chance of survival. We'll get together for a design meeting next week.'

Mollified for the moment, the two men filed out and Olivia Marsden followed them.

Lord Foulridge turned to Nikki before he left.

'Is there anything we can do to help you?'

'Do you think you could talk me through a few points? I'm beginning to realise that I need to know more – a lot more – before I can handle this company.'

Three hours later she was back in her messy office, her head ringing with the information that had been stuffed into it and staring numbly at a huge pile of papers.

She picked up the one on the top of the pile. What did she know about maintenance costs for forklift trucks? And she had no idea if the truly staggering sum demanded for an apparently essential repair was reasonable or not.

The phone at her elbow rang and she let the paper fall, glad of the distraction.

'It's tea-time. Let's have a picnic in the park.'

The warm, deep tone of Alexander's voice sent tingles right down to her toes. Angrily, she quashed this unwelcome reaction. She didn't like the man and she refused to be affected by him.

'Don't you know how much work I've got to get through?'

Silence. Air hummed in the receiver that was trapped against her ear. She wondered what she was waiting for. Why didn't she slam down the phone and get on with her work?

'Nikki, what season is it?'

So often in her dealings with this man she had felt angry and baffled.

'Autumn, of course. What kind of a fool question is that?'

His soft chuckle unnerved her.

'You're not past all hope then, but I'll be surprised if you can answer my next question. What's the weather like today?'

Nikki glanced up at the filthy windows, but could see nothing. She tried to remember what the sky had been like that morning. She'd taken her Labrador for a quick run, but she'd been thinking about work and the climate hadn't registered.

'Go look it up on Teletext!' she snapped.

'Don't you ever relax?'

She spoke with dreadful patience. 'Right now I have work to do and relaxing is not appropriate–'

'Don't you ever just mooch through the park, Nikki, smelling the air and kicking the autumn leaves?'

She looked down at her best kitten heels. 'What? In these shoes?'

She heard him chuckle, but he returned at once to the attack.

'You're always running at full throttle. I wouldn't run a machine like that – it would burn out.'

'I'm not a machine.'

She'd fallen into his trap.

'There you are then. All the more reason to have a walk in the park.'

Oh, he got under her skin!

'Alexander, since you're so keen, please do go for a walk in the park – and get lost!'

She slammed down the phone, regretting her unladylike answer, but it was his own fault for bugging her, and now she was too restless to get down to the piles of work that needed to be done.

She got up from her desk and went over to look at the windows. They were clogged with layers of old paint and cobwebs, but she found a piece of metal and, using it as a crowbar, managed to prise one window open.

Sunlight and crisp autumn air rolled into the room. She could see the blue sky and imagined the smell of apples and roasting chestnuts. It was a beautiful, late October day, and she'd nearly missed it.

A red leaf floated through the air and, to her amazement, landed right next to her on the windowsill. Nikki touched the crimson leaf. It was warm from the sun. Despite all her worries she lingered for a few minutes, soaking up the light and the fresh air. She felt optimistic. She'd soon sort out this factory and be back in her nice, familiar office.

Her phone rang again and she smiled as she went to her desk, carrying the leaf with her. If he asked her again, she would say yes.

'Oh, Nikki, lass. I'm right sorry, I am that.'

Nikki recognised the voice as that of her elderly neighbour. Her stomach clenched, and she felt cold all over as she spoke.

'Mr Hartley? Is that you?'

'Eee, Nikki, I wish I didn't have to tell you this…'

The receiver slipped in her hand and Nikki realised that her palms were sweating.

'I've been burgled? There's been a fire?' Nikki hazarded.

'Oh, Nikki, Marlene's right sorry. She couldn't help it. The dog ran off before she could stop her. You know how she wriggles out of her collar.'

Now Nikki realised that she could hear her cleaning lady sobbing in the background.

'Please, don't tell me. Not Buffy.' Her voice was a whisper.

'I'm so sorry, lass, but it was all over in a minute, the dog ran into the road. A big truck, it was. Poor little Buffy was killed instantly.'

Nikki pressed the phone to her ear and wished with all her heart that she could block out the words she was hearing. Her beloved dog was dead. Buffy wouldn't be waiting in the hall for her when she got home that night.

The thought was unbearable.

She took refuge in practicalities.

'Where is she?'

'The vet took care of her. We thought it for the best.'

The slow shivering in Nikki's stomach turned into a trembling so fierce that she could no longer sit still.

'Thank you for breaking the news, Mr Hartley,' she said quietly. 'Tell Marlene not to worry.'

She banged down the phone and exploded to her feet. She was going to cry. She was going to scream. She hardly registered that the door of her office had opened but somehow Alexander was in the room, smiling.

His voice seemed to come from a different world.

'Nikki, about this bubble wrap–'

He broke off and stared at her. She felt sick and her heart was beating like a drum. But she didn't want him to know what had happened. She felt ashamed to be hurting so much over a mere animal.

She fought to look normal, to make her voice sound steady and light as she asked, 'Have you found a cheap supply?'

Her voice choked. What did she care? An image jumped into her mind. Soft, silly

Buffy, holding her lead in her mouth and thumping her tail as she begged to be taken for a walk.

The realisation that she'd never see Buffy's smiling doggy face again hurt so much that Nikki could hardly breathe. She couldn't maintain her pretence any longer. She turned away and blindly scrabbled for a paper on her desk. The print blurred, but she pretended that she was absorbed in the A4 sheet.

It seemed to take her a long time to find a few words, but finally she managed to say, 'I'm busy. Go away.'

In the silence that followed, she sensed rather than saw the change in his mood.

'What's happened?'

'My dog's been run over, that's all.'

As she said the words, hysteria bubbled up inside her. She lifted her hand to her mouth and bit it, but nothing could stop the storm that was coming. She was terrified. The feeling of losing control was as bad as losing Buffy. But she wasn't going to break down in front of this man.

She had just enough strength to reel past Alexander and totter out of the office. She didn't know where she was going. She let her instincts take over and fled along a dark corridor that came to an end at a massively bolted door. Behind her she heard soft sounds, soothing murmurs that meant nothing. Gentle hands took her shoulders.

'This way. Come with me, Nikki.'

He was so strong, so heart-stoppingly strong, but rather than collapse on his broad shoulders she fought him. Hitting out, kicking, crying great gulping sobs that shook her whole body. She was hardly aware of a door opening and of being pulled into a room. All she knew was that it felt safe inside. The space was dim. Motes of dust hung in the beams of sunshine that were the only illumination. There was soft stuff all around her. Great bales of padding, rolls of bright material, mountains of offcuts.

'Go on,' urged the deep steady voice beside her. 'You're safe in here. No one will know if you cry.'

But Nikki didn't cry. She howled. She raged like a wild thing with the pain and the loneliness and the fear and the fury that whirled around inside her. She was aware of Alexander beside her but somehow his presence didn't seem to matter and when, once the first passion was over, he gathered her close, she let him, turning her head to his chest and sobbing out her pain in the darkness. She could feel his hands on her hair. He made no attempt to stop her tears, but a slow steady sense of calm seemed to emanate from him and wrap around her like a blanket.

Her sobs slowed and then finally stopped. She was aware of her surroundings again. They seemed to be sitting in the centre of a pile of quilted material that was printed with a pattern of storks.

With awareness came shame. She felt broken and vulnerable, and she didn't want him to know that. She tried to get up.

'I'm all right now. Let me go. I have to get back to work.'

'Not while you're so upset.'

'I'm not upset. She was only a dog.'

'It's OK to love your pet, sweetheart. Didn't she love you?'

Huge painful tears welled up in her eyes and slid down her cheeks.

'I'm sorry,' she said.

He held her quite still, and this time she didn't resent the time he took before replying.

He touched her damp cheek thoughtfully.

'Why be sorry for caring?'

She could feel their heartbeats in the silence. A beam of sunlight fell on the edge of their cloth cocoon, lighting up the sweet pattern of storks and fat babies. She lifted her gaze to look at the man who held her.

Alexander's face was very close to her own, and suddenly she realised that it would be a mistake to stay still for even one moment longer. But she didn't move away as his lips travelled towards her in the dimness.

A shock washed over her as he kissed her. She felt as if she'd fallen into a snow-frozen lake in the mountains. For one heady moment she wanted him to kiss her for ever, but then her will asserted itself. Nikki pushed aside the feeling that this man was everything she'd ever wanted and broke the delicious contact with his firm, full lips.

'We can't do this.'

He still held her. Now she was glad that he was taking the time to think before acting. A deep sigh seemed to shake his body, followed by a deep chuckle and an affectionate hug.

'Perhaps not now, anyway.'

Nikki twisted away from him and stood up, brushing at the lint pieces that clung to her black suit.

'Not ever.'

She could feel his hurt in the silence that followed. Her hands shook as she tried to tidy her hair, her clothing. Her throat was dry, her stomach burned, and there was a pounding ache in her temples. She hated crying. Physically it made her feel awful and it had only changed things for the worse.

Poor Buffy was still dead, and now she had to decide how to handle a messy involvement with a man who drove her nuts.

He was infuriating, but he was gorgeous.

The sensory memory of his kiss flamed over her in a golden aftershock. Nikki almost weakened, but a vivid memory flashed into her mind. She saw her mother excusing the hurtful behaviour of her latest young husband, because, 'He makes me feel so wonderful, Nikki, darling.'

The image made her strong. She pushed aside her troubling emotions and set her quick brain to finding a solution; one that would protect her and ensure that she didn't have to feel any more pain and confusion.

She looked directly into Alexander's eyes and spoke with every ounce of free will that was in her.

'I'm sorry. I was upset. I want to pretend that this hysterical outburst never happened, and I want you to do the same.'

She heard his soft breathing in the dim room. His clothing rustled as he stood up. His shadow broke the pattern of sunbeams as he moved through them. Golden sunlight lit his strong face, lighting his brown eyes into amber. She wanted to know what he was thinking, but the expression in his dark pupils was unreadable.

'Have dinner with me, Nikki?'

One tiny part of her heart, deep down, let her know that she wanted to go with him, but she'd built too strong an armour to listen to it. Her protective mechanism snapped back in seconds.

'I don't think that's a good idea.'

Why did she feel a thread of disquiet as she waited for his answer? He only looked at her in a kindly way and gestured towards the door.

'Just as you like.'

Walking into the corridor was like opening a refrigerator door on a hot sticky day. The cool air touched Nikki's flaming cheeks and refreshed her overheated nerves with a touch of reality.

Alexander walked next to her, matching his pace to her own.

She could hear her heels clicking in the quietness.

She didn't know if she wanted to thank him for looking after her, slap him for kissing her, or scream at him for stirring up her emotions so badly. So she said nothing.

The silence between them didn't seem to bother him but as they drew near the main stairwell that descended to the factory floor, he checked his pace and tilted his head to listen.

'The machines have stopped.'

Nikki listened. There was no sound, and now she realised that the normal hum and vibration of the working assembly lines was missing. She turned to Alexander and saw that he was already halfway down the stairs that led to the factory.

Reflecting that he could move fast enough when he wanted to, she went after him, her high heels clattering on the stone steps.

The old-fashioned assembly line was still. Oil dripped from the high chains and pooled on the belts beneath. Nikki's breath caught in her throat.

'Has there been a breakdown?'

Her question was answered by a distant shout.

'Strike! Everybody out! We're on strike!'

4

Strike!

Alexander ran through the silent machinery and made for the big double doors that led to the exit. Nikki followed him out into the cold grey day and was appalled by the ferocity of the scene outside.

Before them a pushing, shoving crowd filled the yard and the air was ringing with shouts and jeers.

Nikki realised that she'd left her mobile phone on her desk in her office. She clutched at Alexander's arm.

'Ring the police!'

'Maybe, but not yet.'

Nikki shut her eyes briefly, but she could still hear the shouts. Why wouldn't he phone the police?

'Alexander!'

He turned his head and looked down at her, seeing her anxiety.

'Let's find out what's going on before we make any hasty decisions.'

He smiled at her briefly, then put a protective arm around her waist.

The main disturbance seemed to be amongst a tightly-packed circle of workers near the main entrance. They looked like a crowd gathered around a fight in a schoolyard.

Nikki made no attempt to escape from Alexander's protective arm as he pushed a way through.

In the centre of the ring of spectators, the clear space was occupied by three figures: a young woman in neat office clothes, a big-bellied bearded worker, and a furious Norman Thompson. His blue suit was rumpled and he was waving his arms and bellowing.

'Cuba! That's the place for communists like you! If you're so keen on the system, why don't you clear off there and leave me to run my factory?'

The bearded man rolled up the sleeves of his overall.

'We've got rights, we have, and you can't go sacking people without consulting with the union.'

'Temporary workers haven't got any rights! You buy them by the hour and if they're useless like this one, you blooming well send them back.'

Nikki saw the young woman wince, and she felt a sudden rush of sympathy as she registered her frightened white face.

'I didn't mean to cause trouble. Just let me go home, please,' the girl, evidently a temporary secretary from an agency, kept saying.

Norman Thompson waved his arms even more furiously.

'Just let her go home! She's no use to me!'

The office temp looked even more distressed and made a movement to leave, but the bearded union man shot out one arm and stopped her.

'You're not going anywhere until I'm satisfied we're following correct procedure here.' His eyes gleamed angrily and his words boomed out.

Norman Thompson whirled on him angrily.

'Correct procedure? Am I the boss or not? I decide what the correct procedure is! And what I say, goes, remember? I'm the boss.'

Nikki felt a cold draught at her side as Alexander moved away from her. His smile was genial, but she heard the warning in his low-pitched tone.

'Actually, Norman...'

The old manager's head whipped around and he faced Alexander as if there was about to be a shoot-out. The two men stood silent under the cold grey sky, their eyes locked. The fight was one of wills alone, but it was real.

Nikki suddenly realised that she was holding her breath. She knew that most of the pram company's management team had left, like rats leaving a sinking ship, but Norman Thompson had clung on to his job. Yet if he had been as much in charge as he claimed, then he was directly responsible for the decline of the factory.

Go on, Alexander, she urged silently, show the old blockhead who's the real boss around here.

It didn't take long. After perhaps only three minutes, Norman Thompson's shoulders seemed to sag, and he shook himself slightly. The battle of wills was decided.

Nikki's breath whooshed out in relief. And then she was surprised by herself. She'd been cheering for Alexander! Yet only a few minutes ago, she'd wanted to fry him in oil.

He was turned away from her now, bending his dark head close to the white hair of the manager. His air was leisurely, as if he had all the time in the world; he seemed to be urging Norman to explain his side of the story.

The workers were milling around for the

sake of movement, excited, longing for something to happen. The man with the beard was haranguing them on the stand that the union should take. The temporary secretary that the rumpus seemed to be about was standing alone, head down, looking miserable.

Nikki tried to remain detached. She had no interest in this row. In fact, if the whole factory went on strike then they wouldn't be able to make the prams for the Middle East and she would have a cast-iron excuse to close it down.

She had decided not to interfere, but then she saw the silver trail of tears on the secretary's cheeks and felt a rush of uncontrollable sympathy. The woman was alone with her trouble, the way that Nikki had been earlier until Alexander had come to comfort her.

Nikki was at the woman's side in a moment. She didn't touch her, that wasn't her way, but she spoke to her as honestly as she could.

'This must be dreadful for you. Can you tell me what happened?'

The temp was about her own age, Nikki saw – twenty-eight or nine. Her blue eyes were miserable, and there was real distress in her voice.

'Oh, why did I leave the supermarket? This

is my first job since I finished my secretarial training. I'd never have come here if I'd known what it would be like!'

Nikki made her tone bracing. 'Ah, but look at it this way: your next job's got to be better!'

The temp looked surprised, and then a smile sprang into life behind the tears. 'I hope so. I didn't intend to cause any trouble, you know.'

'Of course you didn't! What happened?'

The woman recovered herself enough to reach for a handkerchief.

'The temp agency rang me this morning and offered me a job here while Mr Thompson's secretary is off sick. Well, when I got here there wasn't anything for me to do; just one letter to type. Mr Thompson told me to make thirty copies of the same letter and then to post them all first class to the suppliers.' The secretary sniffed. 'All I did was suggest sending the letters by e-mail. I was just trying to be helpful. I couldn't believe he wanted me to copy the same letter thirty times. Anyway, for some reason he went mad, told me I wasn't suitable for the job and to clear off!'

Nikki looked at her face. The woman seemed to be sincere, but there had to be more to the row than her simple explanation.

She sensed rather than heard Alexander behind her, and she moved away so that they could talk privately.

'Can this be true?' she asked him.

His tawny eyes were rueful. 'Norman's a touchy old beggar, and he's very anti-technology. It sounds to me as if she suggested using e-mail and he flew into a rage over it because he doesn't understand it.'

Nikki looked at the yard full of furious, grumbling workers.

'All this trouble because a temp wanted to use e-mail? I can't believe it.'

'His own secretary keeps him sweet and does things the old way. In fact, she may well not know any other way to operate. There isn't even a computer in Norman's office.'

Nikki felt an ironic smile lift her lips.

'It's funny – I've spent all morning complaining to my secretary that she can't take a step without me, and yet this poor girl gets the sack for showing a spark of initiative.'

Nikki looked at Alexander. Rain had begun to fall and scattered drops shone in his thick black hair and sparkled on the ends of his lashes. His tawny eyes were soft and approving. He seemed to know what she was going to say before she spoke.

'A secretary would be useful to me while

I'm here,' she mused aloud. 'Do you think she would work for me?'

Alexander smiled. 'Ask her,' he suggested.

Nikki looked at the gathering of overalled workers.

'Will they go back to work, do you think?'

'I should think so. You go sort out your new secretary and leave me to settle the men.'

Nikki sent her new secretary home for the rest of the day. Tomorrow would be plenty of time to start afresh, and besides, there wasn't a second desk or chair in the office that Nikki was using.

The girl argued a little, wanting to stay and help, but Nikki insisted.

'But I'll see you tomorrow, Linda,' she called, waving the woman out through the factory gates.

The rain fell harder. Nikki shivered. She needed her head examining, standing out in the wet. She clattered across the now empty yard and back into the factory, her heels skidding on the cobblestones that gleamed in the rain.

As she breezed along the corridors, she felt the vibrations of machinery operating. The mill hands must have gone back to work. She realised that she wasn't as surprised by Alexander's efficiency now as she would have been when she first meet him.

Still shivering and feeling cold to the bone, she marched faster and faster down the echoing concrete passage that led to her office, but she couldn't get away from the impact of the experience she'd just been through.

She had never known a day like this for emotional storms. She was exhausted. She was wet and she was freezing. She would pick up her bag and her phone and go home.

But the knowledge that she would have to walk into an empty house twisted her stomach. She ignored the cold burning pain. She would have to face her first homecoming without Buffy eventually, and she was a great believer in getting unpleasant things over with. She would go home.

However, as she pushed open her office door, she saw a pink message slip in the middle of the desk. She didn't believe in telepathy but the very moment she looked at that message slip she knew instinctively what she would find written on it. She hardly needed to look at the note.

Her hand was trembling as she picked up the phone and dialled the nursing home.

'Could I speak to Dr Evans, please? It's Nicole Barton's daughter.'

The doctor's voice was soothing but evasive as he explained the situation.

'Flu could be very dangerous in your mother's condition. But against that risk we have to consider the advisability of using any more antibiotics.'

'What do you mean by advisability?'

Dr Evans' voice buzzed in her ear while he enumerated possible courses of action, listing the pros and cons of each while being careful never to commit himself to recommending any one particular treatment.

Nikki shivered in her damp suit. She rubbed her forehead as she clutched the phone. She wished she had a brother or a sister to help her carry the load, or someone's broad shoulder to rest her head on.

She felt a troubling urge to consult Alexander, but she discounted it. How could he help her when he knew nothing about the situation? But at least he wouldn't talk her head off while she tried to think.

'OK! OK!' she snapped impatiently at the doctor. 'I think you've made it quite clear that I am responsible for any decisions concerning my mother's treatment, and not you.'

The silence that followed was offended, and all too short. Dr Evans moved straight into verbal attack mode.

'Why don't you ever visit her? Perhaps you

would understand the situation a little better if you had first-hand knowledge of her condition.'

Nikki vowed to find another nursing home for her mother as soon as she was fit to be moved. So far as Nikki was concerned, the enormous cheque that she sent every month paid for the understanding that she was never pressurised into visiting that hospital in Wales. She couldn't bear to think of the silent husk who lay there.

Her voice trembled as she replied. 'I can't get away from work just now. Please continue to do all that you can to make her comfortable.'

The doctor sighed. 'Very well, Miss Marlow. But we'll expect to see you very soon, shall we?'

The phone didn't want to go back into its cradle. Nikki knocked it around a few times before the receiver clicked back into place.

Then she sat motionless in her chair and looked straight ahead of her as she tried to decide what needed to be done next. If only her eyes wouldn't sting so. If only her throat wasn't so tight. She willed all the strength she could muster. She knew how to handle pain. The one sure cure was activity. It never failed her.

She glanced at her watch. If she left now, she could catch her favourite step class at the gym near her house.

5

Too Much Chemistry

Nikki felt so much better for going to the exercise class that, at five o'clock the next day, she sent Linda home and reached for her sports bag. From now on, she was planning to call in at the gym every evening on her way home.

However, on her way out of the office her foot clanged against an empty tin that had once held machine oil. She stopped and looked around at the filth and jumble that surrounded her.

Adding a second desk and chair for her new secretary had only increased the chaos. If ever a room needed energy expending on it, this was it. And to turn this scrap heap into a working environment would be a much more worthwhile activity than burning off energy at aerobics.

She looked down at her clothes. She was wearing a suit that she was fond of – she didn't want it ruining. So she decided to change into her sportswear. Leggings and a T-shirt would be much more suitable for furniture moving and cleaning.

Before she got changed, she paid a visit to the packing department.

There was no one around so she helped herself to a roll of black rubbish bags and the biggest cardboard boxes she could carry. She took everything back to her office, got changed, and set to it.

The factory fell quiet around her. It worked to a different rhythm at night. The night shift had been laid off as there wasn't enough work for them, but a skeleton crew kept the essential machines moving.

Nikki shook her head as she stuffed rubbish into the sacks. Why had none of this stuff been cleared away before now? She could understand why some of the items might be kept, the ones that she threw into the cardboard boxes for possible re-use or sale at auction – old clocks and machined parts, a set of brass scales and a nearly new electric sander still in its box; but most of the material she was sorting through was trash! Empty boxes, torn scraps of material, dirty carrier bags, empty oil cans, jars with dried-up nameless gunge in the bottom.

She picked up a rotting box with fungus growing up the sides and wished that she'd brought rubber gloves. But she refused to give up and so she toiled on, steadily filling sack after sack, tying the necks and then standing them out in the corridor until it looked like a city street after a garbage strike.

She was just tying up what felt like her hundredth sack when she heard slow, steady footsteps padding along the corridor outside her room.

She felt heat in her cheeks and wished she wasn't so filthy.

She tried to straighten her blonde hair and realised too late that all she had done was streak it with dirt. She pushed it back impatiently. What did she care what Alexander thought of her, anyway? But she couldn't help noticing that he looked fresh and carefree as he pushed open the door and grinned in at her.

'What did I tell you? We're fashionable again.'

As she met his eyes, Nikki's heart did little flip-flops. She ordered it to be still and concentrated on the piece of paper in his hand instead.

His brown eyes were triumphant. 'We've got another order, for five hundred Windsor prams this time.'

Nikki wished that events would stay still. Now he would probably start angling to keep the factory open. Her head ached at the thought of it.

'It's not a big enough order to change anything,' she told him.

He looked her over for a long silent moment before challenging her.

'Nikki, it's new business; of course it changes things.'

The flash of triumph in his eyes made her feel uneasy, and she realised the mistake she'd just made.

'That is, if we make it at all,' she added quickly. 'I'll take a look at the figures and let you know whether you can start production or not.'

Alexander simply smiled and laid the fax on her desk, saying agreeably, 'Just as you like, Nikki.'

He stood by the desk, glanced at her, and then around the office. She waited for him to leave, but time stretched out and he still seemed absorbed in examining the room.

She bet he went fishing. She could easily imagine him sitting on a river bank staring peacefully into space for hours at a time.

She wanted to get on, but she didn't feel like wading into the rubbish while he was watching her.

'Might I know the results of your meditations?' she asked.

His response was a swift grin. 'You need a man to help you.'

'Who says?' She was furious. She would show him.

She forgot about not wanting to be watched at work, and made for a four-drawer filing cabinet. She had already emptied the drawers and decided where she wanted to move it to. She tipped the big cabinet back and started to wrestle it across the room.

Alexander jumped forward to help her, but she hissed through her gritted teeth: 'I can do it.'

He backed off, but she was aware of him watching her, ready to spring forward if she got into trouble.

His attention made her feel self-conscious and her body was hot and glowing by the time she had the cabinet where she wanted it. She made a few last adjustments to its position and turned to face him. 'You see?'

His grin had softened to a curious look.

'Don't you have a man at home? You seem

very used to coping on your own.'

Nikki wished he would mind his own business and clear off.

'No, I don't have a man at home. I can't be bothered with men.'

'What a waste! You're too cute to be single.'

'And I'm too old and too smart to appreciate being called cute.'

His eyes were very calm. 'How old are you?'

'Can we stop the chit-chat here? I happen to be working.'

'Hmm. I'd say you were about twenty-eight or twenty-nine. Twenty-eight, I'll go for.'

'Very smart.'

'Maybe it's time you did start bothering with men, Nikki. You'll soon be too old to settle down to marriage and babies.'

Nikki was astounded. No one had ever dared venture such a politically incorrect remark to her in the whole of her working life. She could hear herself spluttering before she answered.

'You Neanderthal! I'm a modern woman and I don't need to have a husband and family to feel fulfilled!'

His shrug was leisurely and his eyes were troubled.

'You're right, and I'm sorry. It's because you're so beautiful that I can't believe you're still single.'

Nikki met the appreciative glow in his eyes and for a split second she almost smiled back at him. But only for a split second. Then common sense took hold of her once more.

'Go away, I've got better things to do with my time than flirt with a caveman.'

Disappointment turned his eyes sombre. 'Perhaps we should talk about the feelings between us,' he suggested.

'Get lost!'

Her inelegant response seemed to cheer him up. She saw the flash of white teeth as he gave her a lovely smile.

'I'll help with this mess instead.'

'I don't need help.'

'Everyone needs help sometimes.' There was a soft chuckle in his voice. 'Wouldn't it be nice to be done by midnight?'

Nikki hesitated. It would take her till dawn if she worked on alone, and she hated to leave a job half done.

Alexander looked at a huge wooden reel that had once held thick cable and now took up floor space in the middle of the room He pushed the reel over and started rolling it out.

'Leave it!' snapped Nikki.

He halted at once and straightened up to

look at her. He was much too close. Nikki took a step back. His brown eyes seemed to close the distance between them.

'What's the problem?'

There was no way she was going to admit that she was uncomfortable in his presence. The last thing she wanted was for him to realise how attractive she found him. But knowing she wasn't being entirely truthful made her unwilling to meet his eyes.

She looked away as she answered.

'I don't want to be under any obligation to you. Maybe I should get one of the factory workers to do it in the morning.'

'You'll owe me nothing for this.' His voice was soft and his words came as slowly as ever.

'There's no such thing as a free lunch,' muttered Nikki, but she was tired of arguing and even more tired of the grimy hole that was her office.

So she let him help.

They worked on in silence for about an hour. He went off once or twice to find homes for pieces of not-quite junk they unearthed, but he always came back – which made him nothing like the men that Nikki had been used to at home. None of her mother's young men would have stuck around to paint a wall, let alone work hard on a grimy job like this.

Nor did Alexander take over and try to boss her as she'd half thought he might, considering his nice line in caveman machismo.

The next time he disappeared he came back with the security guard and they were both carrying brown paper carrier bags that smelt wonderful.

'I hope you like Chinese food,' he said.

Nikki's stomach growled and she suddenly realised that she hadn't eaten all day.

'I'm buying,' she insisted.

Alexander studied her face for a long second, then he laughed out loud.

'OK, that's twenty quid you owe me.'

The elderly security guard goggled at him in shock and disapproval.

Alexander grinned back at him, eyes full of mischief.

'We're living in a new millennium now, Dave. The rules are different. The lady can buy me dinner if she wants to.'

Nikki felt defensive. 'It's only right that I buy you dinner. After all, you are helping me clear my office.'

Alexander had given in so easily that she didn't understand why she felt as if she'd lost a point as she hunted for her purse. But then her mouth watered and she resolved to stop worrying. She was ravenous after all the physical effort, and she was grateful for the fragrant, delicious food.

Once the hunger pangs were satisfied, she became aware of him watching her eat.

'What are you looking at?'

'I was just thinking how good it is to see a woman enjoying her food.'

Nikki realised that he'd barely taken two bites and she'd practically emptied her carton. She put down her plastic fork.

'I'm sorry!' he said quickly. 'Don't let me put you off.'

'You haven't. I've finished.'

A frown pleated his brow. 'You don't eat enough. You look like you're losing weight.'

Nikki knew he was right. That morning she'd had to use a belt to keep up her skirt – but her weight was none of his business.

'You're being over personal again,' she warned him as she threw her food wrappers into a rubbish sack. 'I'll make us some coffee if I can use the machine in your office.'

'Coffee? At this time of night? No wonder you're so nervy. I'll have chamomile tea, thank you.'

Nikki made her way down the corridor to Alexander's office. Her whole system cried out for coffee. So far as she was concerned, herbal tea was for wimps who didn't wear leather and sported long hairy beards.

Then she thought of Alexander's solid chin. Whatever his philosophy, Alexander Davidson was far from being a wimp. In fact, in many ways he was the strongest man she'd ever met.

It was just a pity that he always seemed to be opposing her, or sneakily persuading her.

She suddenly suspected that she'd been tricked. Did he think that she'd let him start production on the new order if he helped her clean her office and fed her with Chinese food?

As she spooned fragrant black coffee into the machine, she decided to make her position clear. She was simmering now, almost as fiercely as the coffee machine.

As soon as it was ready she grabbed a drink in each hand and dashed back to her office. The door banged as she charged through it.

'Look! I don't want you getting too excited about that order. We might not even make it. I still don't know why you're so keen to try to keep this hellhole running.'

Alexander lifted his head and regarded her with astonishment that changed into a slow, sad weariness.

'Nikki, it's after midnight. Let's not talk

about work.'

She felt deflated at once.

'Sorry,' she muttered, 'but I was just thinking...'

He held up a large hand.

'Well, don't!' he ordered firmly. 'Let's take it one job at a time. We have a design meeting in the morning. Would you like me to send one of the men in with a steam cleaner to do the floor and windows while the office is empty?'

Nikki looked down at the collection of smears and stains and downright muck that obscured the stone floor.

'That would be great. Do you think there's a surface worth sealing, somewhere underneath the dirt?'

Alexander examined the floor thoughtfully. Nikki had nearly finished her coffee by the time he answered.

'There might be. The flagstones look as if they're in reasonable condition.'

Nikki spluttered with laughter.

'Alexander, you've taken so long to answer that I'd forgotten I'd asked you a question.'

He gave a broad grin and laughter danced in his eyes, and Nikki felt her heart beating faster and a pulse hammered in her throat. Was that caused by the coffee? Or by him?

She lifted her fingers and touched the point where it beat fastest. Then she snatched her betraying hand away and tried to speak lightly.

'Maybe the coffee wasn't such a good idea after all.'

Alexander didn't answer, so she glanced up at him.

What she saw in his eyes took her breath away. He reached out and gently touched the soft skin at the hollow at her throat, just where her fingers had been resting. Right where the disorderly throb of her heart betrayed her.

'Tell me not to kiss you, Nikki.'

She couldn't.

She knew perfectly well that she should tell him to back off, and she knew, too, that he would retreat if she asked him to. But she didn't say a word. Instead, she reached for his strong broad shoulders and wrapped her arms around them, pulling him close to her.

The chemistry was terrific. His kiss touched her heart and his lips were imprinted on her soul. She was flying. She was breathless. She was floating and his strong arms held her safe.

But for all his strength and passion, she felt a caring and a gentleness. She could have stayed in his arms for ever. But then she needed to look at him. She looked into his eyes and tried to read his soul.

His eyes were dark, loving, passionate. Nikki felt her breath coming in shallow wisps. She felt transported, reckless. Magic throbbed in her veins as she waited for him to make the next move. But he merely traced the line of her brow with one gentle finger and when he spoke, his tone was soft and bemused.

'You're not my type. But I guess it won't matter.'

He bent his head gently to kiss her again, but his words had struck Nikki to the core. She felt as if she'd fallen out of paradise and crash landed back on earth. Fear turned her stomach to ice and she knew that she had been saved from a colossal mistake.

She drew back and looked at him sadly. Yes, he was gorgeous. Yes, she could let herself want him, but...

'Alexander, we shouldn't do this.'

He was watching her, his eyes tender.

'I'm not going to make the same mistakes that my mother made.'

He took a step back, settled himself comfortably on Nikki's desk and then sat looking at her encouragingly. His whole demeanour suggested that he was happy to listen to her all night if need be. And his quiet listening expression led her to reveal more than she ever had to anyone.

'The chemistry between my parents was terrific. Mum always said that. She thought it was the only thing that mattered. But Dad always let her down. And the rows ... they were awful. And then Dad ran away.' She stopped, a lump in her throat.

'It can't have been a happy home,' said Alexander gently.

'Mum kept looking for a replacement for Dad. For more great chemistry. For some reason she always married younger men. Younger and younger. But no matter how good the chemistry was, it always ended badly.'

He looked at her with perception in his eyes. 'I understand you better now,' he said.

Nikki laughed ruefully. 'I understand Mum better too.'

Alexander sighed. 'So you promised yourself that you would never make the same mistake. That you would never get involved in messy relationships that could hurt you. You would concentrate on your career.'

Nikki nodded. 'My career is far more important to me than any man could ever be,' she said fiercely. 'I don't need any emotion to muddle the issue here. I want to close down the factory and prove to my bosses that I've handled the situation well. Then they'll offer me a partnership. That's why this madness has to end now.'

Alexander let her move away. He didn't seem surprised by her retreat.

Nikki took a step back and met his tawny brown eyes defiantly. She could feel adrenaline flooding her system. Just let him argue with her! He met her gaze steadily, and once again she had the strange sensation that he was pulling her thoughts out of her mind and examining each one.

She didn't like the feeling at all. She turned away and reached for her coat. 'I'm going home.'

Part of her was piqued when he made no protest.

'I'll walk you to your car,' was all he said.

'Thank you, but that really won't be necessary.'

As usual he didn't reply, but Nikki wasn't surprised that he waited for her while she buttoned her coat over her gym clothes. She let him pick up her suit and her sports bag and said nothing as they started walking along the cold corridors. She was very conscious of him padding along beside her as they reached the dark and empty car park.

A bitter wind scuffed the autumn leaves that rustled around their feet.

'Good night, Nikki.'

His steady brown eyes were grave. Biting her lip and feeling as if she'd been put in her place, she wrenched her belongings out of his arms and threw them on to the back seat of her car. Then she jumped in and gunned the engine.

For the second time since she'd met him, she pulled out of the car park in a spray of gravel and screeching tyres.

Knowing it was weak of her, she still looked in her driving mirror for his reaction. His posture was relaxed, but when did he ever look hurried or angry? She couldn't read his expression; not that she cared what he was thinking, of course.

As she drove through the empty streets, Nikki scrabbled in her glove compartment and slammed a CD into the car stereo. She wasn't going to think about Alexander any more. She sang along to the CD, beating time on the steering wheel, and concentrated on negotiating the steep narrow lanes that led home.

It was true that an empty house waited for

her, but Nikki felt surprisingly cheerful. There was an exceptionally bright moon that evening and as she passed through a sage green plantation of fir trees all frosted with starlight, she felt quite sorry for people who couldn't see how fine they looked.

6

Nikki Takes A Risk

Nikki felt less sure of herself the next morning. Part of her couldn't help feeling that she had been railroaded into holding the design meeting. Why had she agreed to it? There was no sense in discussing new models for a pram factory that was closing down.

She smoothed down her power suit, which was bitter chocolate with gold buttons. She meant to make her presence felt at this meeting.

She was surprised by how familiar she felt with the faces around the boardroom table. She'd been here no more than a week, but already she felt as though she had known Alexander, Lord Foulridge, Olivia Marsden,

Alan Marsh, and even Norman Thompson for ages.

Alexander introduced two unfamiliar faces as the men from the design consultants.

Nikki welcomed everyone to the meeting and then got straight down to business.

'I thought Linda could take the minutes for us, if that's all right with everyone.'

At first, Nikki found herself enjoying their discussion on the progress of the work in hand. Alexander, in particular, was a joy to listen to. He was honest and straightforward in his explanations of how things worked, and he wasn't given to bluff or waffle.

The trouble started when they got on to discussing the new designs, and Norman Thompson spread several drawings over the table. Nikki leaned forward and looked at pictures of a big old-fashioned pram with pink ruffles. It had a pink satin cover, little pink bows and lace frills all over it.

Norman's chest puffed out.

'This is a pram that any lass would be proud to push around the park.'

Nikki looked at the design consultants, wondering what they would say to earn their money, but they maintained a cowardly silence.

Finally Alexander stirred and spoke in his

slow way.

'It's a fine, traditionally styled pram, Norman, but not the sort of thing a modern mum could take on the bus on the way to the crèche.'

Norman Thompson waved his arms as if he was pushing away Alexander's remark.

'It's pink,' he protested. 'Lasses love pink.'

The consultants looked at each other, but said nothing.

It was left to Alexander to comment, 'But it's not just lasses that push prams these days, Norman.'

The older man looked blank.

Alexander's gaze wandered around the other faces at the table, but no other comment was forthcoming, so he shrugged his massive shoulders and explained.

'If I had a child, then I'd want to take it places with me, but not in that pram!'

Norman Thompson was losing his always fragile grip on his temper.

'Real men don't push prams! Prams are for girls, I tell you.'

Nikki was shocked to see the fury that sprang into Alexander's eyes.

She thought he'd blast Norman Thompson out of the room and was amazed when he only said quietly, 'Norman, it's that sort of outdated attitude that has led this company along the road to ruin.'

Norman Thompson banged on the table. His face was as pink as his pram covers and he spluttered like a furious steam kettle.

'Listen to me, I tell you! Throw out these design people and let's make some real prams. Didn't we get a new order yesterday? An order for my prams, hey? How can they be so bad if people are ordering hundreds of them? Tell me that!'

Alexander took his usual time about answering.

'That order came from a part of the world where the old stereotypes hold good. They will continue to buy our classic prams, and I think they would like your concept in pink.'

Triumph blazed in Norman Thompson's eyes. 'Well then?' he demanded.

Alexander regarded him steadily. 'But I also think that you'll find the home market has changed.'

'Stuff and fancy nonsense! Rubbish! My prams are as good as ever they were!'

'No one's disputing that, Norman.'

'Well then, why do you want to go mucking about with new designs?'

'Fashions change. The market has moved on.'

'Oh, I haven't the time to be listening to this rubbish of yours! I've a good mind to clear off back to the factory floor and leave you all to it.'

Alexander nodded his head slowly. 'Please minute that, Linda,' he said.

Norman Thompson was aghast. His jaw dropped open and his faded blue eyes darted frantically around the room, looking for a friendly face.

But nobody urged him to stay at the meeting. In fact nobody moved, until Lord Foulridge took off his glasses and polished them, giving a gentle cough before speaking.

'The board is most appreciative of all the sterling work you have contributed over the years, Norman, but times change. Alexander is correct in what he says.'

The old man sprang to his feet.

'I've worked for this firm for thirty years and this is how you treat me? Throwing me out of a board meeting?'

His elderly blue eyes met Nikki's. The venom in them made her recoil.

'You're the only one here with any sense! You were right all along. Shut the place down!'

Nikki felt an unpleasant jolt as the old man's furious eyes bored into her. For the very first time she doubted her decision to close down the factory. She didn't want to be on Norman Thompson's side. She had no sympathy for his ideas whatsoever.

Every face in the room was turned to her, and she could feel people waiting for her answer. For once it didn't come quickly.

'Closure is not a decision I would recommend lightly,' she said at last.

Thompson jumped to his feet and pointed straight at her.

'You've changed your tune, eh, lass? Been got at, have you? Someone's lined your palm with silver, have they? I bet your bosses won't be too pleased to hear about this.'

Nikki rocked in her seat as if the old man had hit her with his fist rather than with words.

Alexander sprang like a tiger. He rose to his full height and spoke in a voice that filled the room.

'I think you'll agree, Norman, that you should apologise to Miss Marlow and that your contribution to this meeting is at an end.'

His words were mild, but the tone was one that Norman Thompson couldn't withstand. He sneaked one look at Alexander and then his gaze fell to the floor.

'Sorry,' he muttered. Then his anger bubbled up afresh and he picked up his designs and tore them corner to corner. Pink and white scraps of paper floated across the table and fluttered to the floor as he slammed out of the room.

Alexander resumed his seat as calmly as ever and smiled benignly around the table. Nikki marvelled at his composure as he spoke to the red-headed engineer.

'Alan, I'd like you to tell us about the engineering concepts behind your new undercarriage design.'

Nikki was still breathless from the emotional storms that had shaken the room, but she knew how to force aside troubling issues and focus on work. She'd done it many times before, and this time it was easy.

As Alan Marsh showed them his idea for a pram wheel system that would easily negotiate bus steps, kerbstones and pavements, she soon got drawn in. She could see the potential at once. His drawings were for lightweight buggies of a modern design. Cute, fun, flexible and modern, they were everything that the old Davidson prams were not. They would sell, she was sure of it.

'If – and it is only if at this stage! *If* I give the go ahead, what's the next step?' she asked Alan.

The young engineer looked painfully eager. 'Next, we knock up some prototypes in time for the Harrogate Baby Carriage Fair. It'll be tight for time, but I think we can do it. It's the first event of the New Year. All the major European retailers place their orders at that fair, so if we're not ready by then, the game's over.'

'For ever,' Nikki pointed out, and a gloomy silence fell.

Nikki picked up her pen and twirled it between her fingers. Her stomach growled. Her chest burned. Her indigestion was bad again today.

She could feel the tension around the room. She was aware of people watching her; of Lord Foulridge's steady gaze and Olivia's sympathetic smile. Alexander she didn't dare look at, but she could feel his eyes on her. Was her attraction to him warping her judgement?

The wooden clock in the corner ticked on. She knew people were waiting as she scribbled down all the relevant figures, but she refused to be pushed into an answer. She tapped her pen restlessly on top of her calculations. She couldn't sell up much before the first week in January, even if she wanted to. Everyone deserved a chance, and the factory was losing so much money, what harm could it do to gamble a little bit more?

'We'll go ahead!' she announced.

'Yes!'

'Thank you, Miss Marlow.'

'How perfectly splendid!'

'Well done, my dear, I'm sure that's the right decision.'

Alexander said nothing, but Nikki couldn't help looking at him and the joy and approval that she saw in his eyes was like a sunburst around her heart. The emotion that she was feeling overwhelmed her, and as usual she took refuge in activity.

'Organise some focus groups to discuss these designs at once.'

The design consultants nodded their heads and went away happy.

'Alan, you can start work on the samples as of now.'

'Wowee! That is, thank you, Miss Marlow!'

The engineer winked cheerily at Linda, then marched through the door, whistling.

'Does this mean you're putting the closure plans on hold?' Lord Foulridge asked hopefully.

'Absolutely not! But it's going to take until the New Year to value the factory anyway, so

I'm going to keep on with that process. If the new prams set the world alight, then fine. The inventory will help us know where we are and to plan for the future. But I'm afraid that Harrogate is the last chance. If we make no sales, then I'm closing the factory.'

Lord Foulridge nodded his silver head.

'That's fair, I suppose. In fact, it's extremely good of you to give the establishment one last opportunity to redeem itself.'

Olivia Marsden agreed with Lord Foulridge and as she followed him out of the boardroom, she turned to speak to Alexander.

'It's up to you now, Alexander. I know you'll make the place a success.'

Oh, so it's all up to the man, is it, thought Nikki.

Once the other board members had left the room, she turned to give Alexander a simpering look from under her lashes.

'You'll have to move quickly, Superman! Only nine weeks to save the factory!' Her tone was more vinegar than honey.

He merely lifted his thick dark lashes and slowly blinked at her.

'I'm on your side this time!' she cried sharply. 'How can you argue with that?'

He lifted one eyebrow and looked at her

ironically. His tawny eyes were as dangerous as a lion's.

'Am I arguing?' was all he said, but the sarcasm in his tone infuriated her.

'For once, no, you're not. But while we're on the subject of arguing, it was very macho of you to leap to my defence when Norman Thompson started yelling at me, but I'll extract my own apologies and fight my own battles in future, thank you!'

Alexander's eyes narrowed to sleepy slits with just a gleam of light between them. Nikki's mouth went dry and she could feel her heart pounding. For all his air of slow and sleepy gentleness, there was a quality in this man that made it difficult for her to oppose him. But she was right, and she knew it.

He looked at her for a long moment before heaving himself to his feet.

'Just as you like, Nikki.'

Nikki jumped up, furious with him.

'I think we need to get a few things straight between us–' she began to say before Alexander held up a warning hand and spoke to Linda.

'That's all for now, thank you, Linda.'

The secretary left. They were alone in the wood-panelled boardroom.

Nikki drew a deep breath.

'I want to sack Norman Thompson,' she announced.

Alexander stroked his chin and said nothing.

'He does nothing but cause trouble,' she explained.

Alexander looked at her thoughtfully but said nothing.

'For goodness' sake, Alexander! It's his fault that this place is so rundown. What's your problem with getting rid of him?'

Alexander didn't answer and she turned on him furiously.

'Alexander! Can't you see how much trouble the man causes?'

'Well, yes, but you know he's due to retire in four months?'

She'd been so right to fight against her attraction for this man. He might have been a six-legged blob from outer space so far as his thought processes were concerned. They would never get on.

'What's that got to do with anything?' she asked him.

'Nothing, because you're closing down the factory before then.'

Nikki felt as if her nails were scraping down a pane of unbreakable glass while she screamed fruitlessly behind it. She had never come up against such an immovable force.

Abruptly she gave up. Her head had suffered enough for one morning.

'I'll see you later,' she told him. 'I'm too busy for this.'

She knew that he knew she was running away, but she simply didn't care at this point. She wanted to get away to somewhere quiet, take an indigestion remedy and then get on the phone to Marie. She needed to remind herself that she had another life where she wasn't presented with these endless dilemmas. She missed her old life at Bosworth's with an intensity so sharp that it was a pain in her heart.

But it seemed that Bosworth's were not missing her. Nikki listened uneasily as Marie listed account after account that she'd passed on to someone else.

'You do have a shining talent in one direction, at least, Marie. I've never met anyone like you for delegation.'

Her secretary's reply was uncertain. 'Is that a compliment? I'm only following procedure, Nikki. When someone's on an insolvency case, we always share out their work around the office.'

Nikki knew that. She'd acquired some of her best accounts by exploiting the absence of others. She supposed she would have to fight her corner again when she returned, but the issue seemed curiously distant.

'That's fine, Marie. I'm glad that my absence is causing no problems.'

'Oh, no one's missing you at all. Have you remembered about Brenda's party, by the way? Will you be there? It's tonight, at the Cupid Club.'

It was on the tip of Nikki's tongue to say she couldn't make it. But then she changed her mind.

'Do you know,' she said to Marie. 'I'm longing to see everyone. I feel like I've been exiled in the Siberian salt mines, working in this place. A party is exactly what I need. I'll be there, and I'm in the mood to boogie!'

7

Nikki Keeps Busy

When Nikki's alarm clock went off the next morning, she wondered how she could have been so stupid. She hurled the offending clock across the room and rolled over into her pillow and groaned. Her hair smelt of cigarette smoke but it was beyond her just yet to make it into the shower to wash off the smell. Physically she'd never felt so ill, and mentally she was pushing aside the knowledge that she hadn't enjoyed herself at the party at all.

She had drunk too much because she'd felt like the single solemn jackdaw at a budgerigar's tea party. She'd been unable to concentrate on the petty office gossip and trivial in-jokes that had flown around the noisy night club. She'd wanted to talk shop, she realised now. She'd been hoping that someone from Bosworth's would give her sage advice that would magically solve the problems that beset her at Davidson's, but as soon as she'd met up with her colleagues she'd known she was dreaming. Inexperienced, out for a good time, the younger members of the office were not people who could advise her on weighty issues.

Nikki had drowned her disappointment with cocktails but she was paying for it now and only made it to work on time through sheer force of will.

Before getting out of her car, Nikki glanced in her driving mirror and was horrified at the image she presented. Her blonde hair was limp and lifeless and her grey eyes were full of pain.

She scrabbled in her bag and managed to open her blusher, but her fingers were alarmingly shaky and unwieldy around the brush.

'Never mind,' she muttered to herself, squinting as she stepped out of the car into the cold October light.

When Nikki reached her office, Linda was already at her desk.

'Good morning, Miss Marlow. Isn't it nice in here now? I never thought it could look like this.'

'Sure, sure. Where are my health salts?'

Alexander walked in as Nikki was draining the last of the fizzing glassful.

'That stuff's bad for your stomach,' he said absently, then he did a double take and stared at Nikki with horror in his brown eyes.

'Great suffering tambourines, woman! You're not well! Go home at once!'

'I'm fine,' she said sourly.

She shifted uneasily as he inspected her more closely. His concern evaporated to be replaced by heard-hearted amusement.

'I diagnose the morning after the night before. How about a nice raw egg for breakfast? I'll whip you one up with Tabasco sauce.'

Nikki immediately felt even worse but Alexander wasn't done yet.

'If you don't fancy that, come down to the canteen and have a lovely greasy bacon sandwich. I'll treat you.'

'Stop tormenting me. I'll be fine in a minute.'

'You don't look fine. You look awful. I hope the party was worth it.'

Nikki felt all her usual anger with the man, but for once she welcomed it. The adrenaline was clearing her head.

'It'll take more than one late night to slow me down! I'm ready for work now.'

His eyes were oddly wistful.

'I wish I had your energy.'

She had to smile as she imagined him clubbing. His calm, casual, unhurried air wouldn't look right in the frantic noise and boom of the Cupid Club. He'd be more at home on a yacht with white sails. He'd be happy spinning over the ocean. A picture rose in her mind, so vivid that she could smell salt and hear gulls calling. He was a man in harmony with nature, and just to look at him annoyed her. He was too fresh and happy, and too healthy by far.

'Go away!' she snarled.

He gave her an unrepentant grin.

'Not until I've had your opinion on these figures.'

He thrust a sheaf of papers at her.

Nikki's fingers trembled as she spread the pages of projections across her desk. Her head felt thick and she had to admit that her hangover was making it difficult to concentrate, which was annoying because Alexander's ideas were interesting. If he was right, this company could fly.

Nikki's stomach burned and her vision blurred, forcing her to stop thinking about Alexander's plans. She felt so awful and the party simply hadn't been worth it. Truthfully, she'd been bored. Maybe she was getting too old for nightclubs.

That was a horrible thought. How would she sleep if she didn't go for a few drinks after work? She had always suffered from insomnia. She went clubbing a lot because she hated lying awake staring at the ceiling, alone with her thoughts.

Pure terror washed over her at the thought of long empty nights at home without even Buffy for company. If she didn't go partying, what would she do with her free time when she wasn't working? Evening classes? Basket weaving at the Women's Institute? She didn't think so.

Nikki turned to Alexander, meaning to say something about work, but as she looked at his big strong body, she suddenly imagined settling down with him.

She could see herself walking along the beach with him, cuddling up on a squashy sofa, tucking in a rosy-cheeked child. The image was so sharp, and so shockingly attractive, that it scared her.

She pushed aside the papers, containing his plans for the factory, so violently that they fell to the floor and scattered. She didn't apologise.

'Look, I'll get back to you later about these,' she told him.

His soft voice was adamant. 'You might as well go home, Nikki. You can't work today.'

She could always do her work! She was a professional. His criticism hurt her, especially as any normal day at Bosworth's began with most of the men complaining of hangovers. It was an accepted part of the culture – for males.

'I suppose you think women should spend their lives sitting at home watching paint dry,' she grumbled.

His answer was strong and sharp.

'Getting drunk in nightclubs isn't living. Are you going to go through your life in an alcoholic blur? It'll be over and you won't know what you've missed.'

She rounded on him indignantly. 'It's my life and I'll party if I want to!'

His eyes were a fathomless peat-coloured pool that drew her unwillingly towards them.

'What are you after, Nikki? What do you want out of life?'

His simple question triggered a red alert deep in her mind. A confused tangle of truths and deeply buried emotions threatened to surface. She instantly slammed down the lid on them, but the feelings didn't go away as easily as they usually did. The burning sensation that had smouldered under her ribs all morning radiated out into her back and chest. She was furious with him for challenging her, and for making her feel worse.

As he looked down at her, the memory of the kiss they'd shared seemed to flame into life between them. Nikki felt dizzy with longing. Lightning seemed to flicker along her nerves. She turned away abruptly. She was weak from her hangover, that was all. She hated being made to feel weak.

'Alexander, I've told you. Go away, give me peace.'

He sauntered away unhurriedly.

'How do you like your new office, Linda?'

he asked, on his way past the secretary's desk.

'It looks really different! Thank you! Nikki said she'd never have got the place sorted without your help.'

His grin was all wickedness as he glanced across the room. 'I never thought Nikki would admit that I was any use at all.'

Nikki opened her mouth to blast him. Then she read the unadulterated enjoyment on Alexander's face. He was playing her like a fish, expecting her to shout at him again. She resolved to surprise him.

'Why, I do declare, Mr Davidson, I just don't know where I'd have been without your wonderful male muscles. It was perfectly darling of you to help me.'

Linda's startled look held pure bemusement, but Alexander's smile was full of appreciation and there was a definite chuckle in his voice.

'That's my girl! I'll come back later, Nikki, when you've had a chance to look over those figures in peace.'

In fact, he left it for several days. Linda said she'd heard that a crisis had blown up at his other factory.

Nikki missed him more than she would ever have admitted. Irritating he might be, but he was also strong and supportive. Nikki wouldn't have liked to handle an emergency without him.

Fortunately, work at the Baby Carriage Company chugged along without any immediate problems and she was able to concentrate on the inventory.

Despite the new orders, the factory still wasn't operating at full capacity so she set several workers to sweeping and cleaning and tidying.

Then she remembered that she had decided the factory would soon be demolished and she set two more men on to hunting out and renovating anything that might go for a good price at auction.

She tried to keep herself so busy that she didn't have time to wonder why she was running the place in this schizophrenic fashion.

Sometimes she thought that Alexander might be right and that the factory could make money again, but as she dug deeper into the accounts the muddle and mismanagement that she found there discouraged her dreadfully.

She grew more and more worried as she begun to understand the true enormity of the gulf between the company as it was, and how it would have to be to become successful.

She'd been a fool to let Alexander talk her into trying to save the place, and when she saw him she would tell him so.

But when his massive figure finally strolled into her office, and she looked up to see his calm face and smiling eyes, she felt a frightening rush of gladness that blew over her like the first wind of spring.

She stamped it down at once and turned away, hoping her feelings didn't show on her face. She tried to sound casual.

'Well, look who's here! What brings you back into town, stranger?'

'The suspicion that you might knock down the factory if I left you here on your own for too long.'

Nikki met his laughing brown eyes and shivered all over in shock and surprise. Desire rose in her blood like nectar. He was a great big gorgeous bear of a man. She longed to throw herself into his arms and cuddle up into his chocolate-brown fleece sweater. She had never known such passion. Was she turning into her mother?

A memory rose before her like a spectre. She could literally see Nicole Barton dropping ice cubes into her gin with shaking hands, snapping impatiently at her small daughter: 'You'll understand when you're older, Nikki darling.'

But Nikki had never been able to understand why her mother kept excusing the bad behaviour of her young husbands.

Nikki had vowed that her own life would be different. And she meant to keep that vow.

'Seriously, I'm glad you're back, Alexander. The results of the marketing exercise are in and the response was very encouraging, but we need to firm up the colour schemes and find a theme for the new range.'

He seemed to examine her face for about half an hour before answering.

'I've been thinking about that. Our new range is light and sporty. How about naming it after famous events like Ascot or Wimbledon? Do you think people would like the Burleigh Buggy?'

As he spoke, he drew up a chair to Nikki's desk. She tensed, waiting to be overwhelmed by his size and his warmth and his masculinity. Then she relaxed. She felt nothing. Her well-trained brain was pushing down her puzzling and frightening reactions, leaving her free to focus on work. She was in control again.

'Great concept!' she said enthusiastically. 'We'll take it to the next design meeting.'

They moved through the list of questions she had compiled while he was away, working together easily, until Nikki asked him, 'How did you get on at your other factory? Did you bring back any fabric samples?'

There was a longer pause than usual, even for Alexander. She looked up and into his face. A thrill shot down to her toes when she met the intensity in his brown eyes. His expression flared with triumph, and when he finally spoke it was with soft pleasure.

'You cared enough to find out where I went.'

Nikki's mouth dried and her carefully contrived illusion of control blew apart. The feelings had been there all the time, and now they were back in full force, roaring through her system like floodwater after a thaw. She couldn't speak. She literally could not speak. All her awareness of him as a man snapped back into her consciousness. A blithe lie or a casual shrugging off of his remark was as far beyond her as flying to the moon. She simply stared at him and drank in the sensation of being close.

It was such a crazy mixture. Peace and comfort seemed to flow from him. There was a feeling of safety that had snapped into place the moment he walked into her office, yet at the same time her whole body burned with a delicious feeling of danger. She shivered all over as the contradictions shook her. She knew she should leap to her feet at once and get away from him before it was too late. But her kitten-heeled shoes were nailed to the floor, and he was still looking at her with warm brown eyes that held the universe inside them.

Nikki turned her head away, breaking the mystical connection that was trying to form between them, and stared blindly at the paper in her hand. Black marks squiggled over the white surface and she pretended she was fascinated by them. In the long silence that followed, the rapid cadence of her heart had time to wind down until it was ticking along close to its normal rate once more. Close, but not exactly.

Five minutes passed. She couldn't imagine any other man waiting so patiently for her response. She turned her head toward his, and there was a kind of desperate frankness in the words she finally granted him.

'Yes, I did ask where you'd gone to, but I'm in charge here, remember? It's my business to know where everybody is. Don't you think there was anything personal in it, because there wasn't.'

Having stated her position, she dared to meet his eyes. His gaze was long, calm and measuring.

'Relax, Nikki. What is it that's scaring you so much?'

She didn't dare think about that. Her gaze fell to the work that was heaped on her desk, and she was grateful for the diversion.

'There's so much to do if we're to be ready for the show. We have to work together. Nothing must spoil that.'

He thought this over slowly. Nikki was glad that he didn't push her.

'Well, maybe you're right.'

Nikki tried to sound businesslike, but a flame burned in her heart, making her aware of the lies that she was mouthing.

'I know I'm right. There's nothing between us. I want you to promise to stop flirting with me and concentrate on work until the proto-types are ready.'

His gaze was level.

'I wasn't flirting, Nikki.'

The shock of his words jolted her down to her toes. Not flirting? What did he think was happening between them? She longed to ask him.

Her mouth trembled but she summoned every ounce of steel that was in her and refused to snap at the tempting bait that he offered.

'Work! We must talk about nothing but work!' she insisted.

He gazed at her reflectively and she thought he was going to challenge her, but then Alan Marsh walked in with a query for him and the moment was gone.

Nikki forced her mind back to business and told it to stay there, but she found it difficult to concentrate. Whenever Alexander was near she was aware of simmering tension swirling between them, even though he behaved impeccably.

A few days before Halloween, Linda asked Nikki, 'Would you like to come trick or treating on Saturday? It'll be a good do.'

'Pardon?' asked Nikki, momentarily baffled by the invitation.

'It's Halloween. My daughter and her friends are trick or treating, and there's a party afterwards at my house.'

Nikki didn't have to look to know that there was nothing but business engagements in her diary.

'Thanks, but I've got something on.'

Her secretary smiled at her with guileless blue eyes and then went back to the letter she was typing.

'That's a shame,' she said. 'Alan Marsh is coming and so is Alexander. I can't wait to see them in fancy dress.'

As Nikki curled up on her sofa with a magazine on Saturday evening, she wondered why she hadn't accepted her secretary's invitation.

Gangs of giggling children knocked on her door all evening. The togetherness of the playful groups was painful in a way that Nikki found hard to analyse as she handed out sweets and oranges. Apart from clubbing after work, she had never wanted friends or a social circle. Why was there a hole in her life now? Why did she feel so lonely? Did everyone who lost a pet feel this horrible uneasy emptiness?

Well, whatever the cause of the complaint, she knew the remedy – work. The one sure cure that never failed. She vowed to work harder than ever. To so immerse herself in business that she could think of nothing else. But before she could get into a good working rhythm, Albert Davidson died.

8

A Sad Day For All

The funeral was set for the fifth of November. The factory was officially closed for the day but Alexander made it clear that attendance at the service was voluntary. The workers were free to spend the time as they wished but every single one of them chose to pay their last respects, and many brought their partners.

Emotion tightened Nikki's throat as she surveyed the packed church.

The windy streets had been lined with sad faces and, despite the freezing November chill, the hundreds of people who couldn't get into the church thronged the cold, grey churchyard outside.

Not wanting to push in, Nikki had waited out there herself, but Alan Marsh had come from the church to look for her and had ushered her into the pew where the rest of the factory's management team were seated.

Nikki broke off her gloomy reflections

when she saw that Alan and Linda were holding hands. Well, good for them! She had come to like her secretary rather a lot.

Flowers, music, eulogies. The memorial service passed in a blur for Nikki. She couldn't feel too sad for a man she had never met, and yet she was troubled by a kind of lingering melancholy that she finally realised was for herself.

Would six local choirs and a brass band turn out to her funeral?

Would the front rows be packed with her grieving family?

Would hundreds of people crowd eagerly around a crackling loudspeaker outside the church because they couldn't get in and they didn't want to miss a word of her send-off?

The speeches were endless. Quite apart from building the factory, it emerged that Albert Davidson had supported just about every good cause within a hundred-mile radius, and person after person rose to bear witness to his good works and sweet nature.

By the end, Nikki was crying openly.

As she followed along behind everyone else out of the church, she reflected that at least Albert had lived a full life and a successful one. His family and many others would miss him, but the good memories would eventually balance out the pain of loss.

And now she understood something of Alexander's determination to keep Davidson's Baby Carriage Company open. It was Albert's memorial.

Despite the cold wind and the length of the service, there seemed to be even more people outside then when Nikki had gone into the church. She didn't try to get anywhere near the graveside, but she did end up standing where she could watch Alexander. She had never seen him in a suit and formal overcoat before. He could never look urbane or sharp, but he did look handsome and solid and safe. The wind that sliced through the cemetery ruffled his dark hair, but he seemed impervious to the cold as he moved unhurriedly through the big crowd, thanking people for coming and directing many to the meal that was being held in a nearby hotel.

Nikki was fascinated to see other members of Alexander's family on the same mission. They looked nice, but she was too shy to speak to any of them. The men's poise and assurance and the women's clear eyes and rose-petal skin told her that these people had never lived the kind of unstable life that the young Nikki had. They looked solid, established and rich.

She couldn't help watching closely as Alexander bent to kiss an elegant, sun-tanned woman with beautifully styled grey hair. A few pretty tendrils had escaped from her French pleat and curled out in the wind. Nikki felt hollow with longing as she watched Alexander tenderly wind a lock around his finger and laugh.

She was his mother, of course. Her bright hazel eyes were lighter in colour, but they were exactly the same shape as Alexander's. But even without the giveaway physical similarities, the closeness between them was unmistakable. He seemed to be shooing his mother off to the hotel, and after a few token protests she allowed him to usher her over to one of the big black funeral cars.

The crowd took ages to disperse, but still Nikki lingered. It wasn't until just about everyone else had left and she saw Alexander looking lost standing next to a stone angel, that she finally admitted to herself that she couldn't leave until she'd spoken to him.

She crossed the frozen ground and stood next to him. His size made her feel delicate. He looked down at her, sombre in his black suit, and she saw that his eyes were dead.

He spoke mechanically. 'It was so nice of you to come. Won't you come to the Metropole for something to eat?'

No wonder he didn't seem to be feeling the cold! The expression in his eyes told her that his heart was frozen solid!

'Alexander, it's me,' said Nikki, feeling foolish, but knowing she couldn't bear for him to talk to her in this blank and empty manner.

A distant light dawned in his eyes as he looked down at her, but it was faint compared with the attention she was used to, and she knew that most of his mind was elsewhere.

'Alexander, you're freezing and everyone's gone. Why don't you come to the hotel with me?'

He rounded on her with such suddenness that she took a startled step back.

'What do you care? You've made that very plain,' he snapped.

'If a fight will make you feel better, then I'm happy to oblige.'

His lips lifted in a wry grin at her response, warming the unnatural woodenness of his expression. Nikki's heart soared as she saw that she had got through to him. She didn't stop to ask herself why she wanted to, or why she was on a one-woman mission to make him feel better.

'Do you want me to come to the hotel

with you?' she asked.

He touched her arm gently while he took his usual time about replying.

'Thank you, Nikki, but no. I'm not going. Everyone will want to talk about Albert.'

Nikki didn't know how to answer him because there was so much she didn't know about him, including how he had felt about his uncle. Rather than say the wrong thing, she joined Alexander in his silence. The wind whined in the tops of the ancient yew trees and whirled around the grey stone church. She shuddered under the cold blast, but the conviction that this man needed her was so strong that she held her place by his side. He seemed to stir himself at last, and placed a warm arm around her waist.

'Nikki! You're freezing to death out here!'

She couldn't stop a small, instinctive movement that had her nestling in towards his warmth.

'So are you,' she told him.

He looked around the now deserted churchyard and his eyes were empty and lost. Nikki made the suggestion impulsively.

'Have you eaten today?' she asked him. 'Because if you're hungry, I'll cook.'

Surprise flared in Alexander's eyes.

'You cook?'

'I drive too. If you truly don't want to go to the hotel, I'll take you back to my place.'

He seemed relieved to have this option laid out before him.

'Please, I'd like that.'

It was so good to get inside the shelter of the car! Nikki turned her heater on full and revved the engine until it warmed up.

After a glance at Alexander's troubled face, she hunted through her CD collection for some soothing Mozart.

They travelled to Manchester in total silence and let the clarity of the music do the communicating for them.

She had parked and turned off the engine before Alexander finally seemed aware of his surroundings.

'This is a long drive for you every day, Nikki.'

'It's only temporary,' she reminded him.

His depression seemed to return.

'Of course – I'd forgotten that,' he murmured.

He was surprised by the interior of her house, gazing at its shabby homely comfort in wonder.

'I'd formed a picture of you surrounded by stainless steel and lots of white surfaces.'

He smoothed the tartan rug that cosied up

her big sofa.

'This is Buffy's house really,' said Nikki sadly, leading the way through to the kitchen. There was still a basket in one corner and paw scratches all over the wooden floor.

'I had to spend so much to get a house next to the park that I didn't have anything left for decorating. It's still rather doggy, but I haven't had the heart to clear it up.'

He didn't rush in with easy words of sympathy, but he gave her a smile that was infinitely comforting and asked her, 'Will you get another dog?'

She shook her head. 'Not while I'm at work all day. It wouldn't be fair.'

Alexander settled himself on one of the kitchen stools and seemed content to chat about the joys and difficulties of puppy rearing while Nikki raided her freezer and all of her cupboards for ingredients. He watched her assembling a shepherd's pie with interest.

'You're a woman of unexpected talents, Nikki. Did your mother teach you to cook?'

Nicole Barton had hated to cook. For a minute Nikki thought she would blurt out one of the many bitter anecdotes that burned inside her, but then she found that she wasn't feeling her usual anger, but only a faraway sadness. She even managed a rueful smile.

'My mother could just about manage to open a packet and operate the microwave. I guess I had to learn to cook in self-defence.'

Alexander gave her that mind-reading look that he seemed to specialise in, but he changed the subject to television cooks and they chatted easily about recipes until dinner was ready.

'And sticky toffee pudding to follow,' he said, pushing aside his empty dish in total satisfaction. 'That was the perfect comfort meal, Nikki. Thank you. You just about saved my life.'

They took their mugs of coffee into the lounge. Nikki lit the gas fire and curled up on the sofa, while Alexander took the squashy chair. He filled it more than anyone else who had ever sat in it.

'I'm sorry I haven't any herbal tea.'

His eyes were warm and appreciative.

'This is fine. Do you mind if I take my tie off?'

'Make yourself comfortable.'

Nikki found the silence restful as they drank their coffee. The grey light from her big bay window seemed to fade away as the orange glow of the fire grew stronger. She glanced at the little gilt clock that ticked busily on the mantelpiece. It was only three o'clock, but the pale November light was fading already.

'Alexander, won't your family mind you not turning up at the hotel?'

She envied the serenity in his eyes, the confidence in his voice, the way that he didn't have to pause before answering.

'They'll understand. It hit me a bit hard today.'

'Were you close to your uncle?'

This time he thought a little longer before replying, glancing up at her face and away as he hunted for the right words.

'It's the contrast that upset me. He's left me the factory, and I suppose I'm the head of the family now, but I can remember when Uncle Albert was king. I used to love the pram works when I was young. It was a wonderful place then. The order books were full, he employed over a thousand people, and the atmosphere was full of life and excitement. It was Uncle Albert's pride and joy.

'I'm glad he's been too frail to understand much, these last few years. It would have upset him to see the business in such a state.'

Nikki shifted restlessly as she pictured the dreadful factory.

'Alexander, I really hate to say this, but I can't believe it can ever be saved.'

135

'Let's not talk about business now, Nikki.'

His brown eyes looked steadily into hers, and Nikki felt something deep and emotional catch in her throat. The room seemed to grow darker and golden shadows played over his face. He said nothing, she said nothing, but passion flickered in the corners of the room and spiralled around them. She was hardly surprised at all by a loud explosion outside. It was followed by a bright white light. Alexander's eyes never left her face.

'Fireworks tonight,' he said softly.

Her mouth dried before she remembered it was November the fifth. Guy Fawkes night. Two more explosions rattled the windows and two silver streaks with fiery comet's tails whistled through the sky. The official firework display must have begun.

Nikki jumped to her feet. She knew she couldn't run away from the feelings that were building inside her, but she crossed the room on shaky legs and went to stand by her window, which overlooked the park.

Brilliant stars pierced the navy blue sky and the glow of a freshly-lit bonfire turned the tops of the trees bright orange. The wind blew sparks across the grass.

Cold air flowed from the big window pane and Nikki wrapped her arms around herself, but she couldn't stop her heart beating faster. This time the silence was searing. Was he fighting temptation, as she was? Her nerve endings knew it when he moved. He came up behind her and circled his strong arms around her, pulling her into his body. She fitted just neatly under his chin. She was so close to his chest that she felt the vibrations when he spoke.

'I didn't come here for this, Nikki.'

'I know.'

He turned her gently and cradled her face with both hands, holding her so that he could look deeply into her eyes. Then he kissed her with a kind of abandon that she would never have expected from him. They held each other tighter and tighter. She was gasping. Fresh explosions outside the window only echoed the tumult in her mind. He kissed her eyelids. He kissed her throat.

'Nikki, you're so beautiful,' he murmured.

Through half-closed eyes Nikki saw rockets whooshing past the window and exploding in a dazzling array of stars against the night sky. There was a wildness to the night that was whipping her senses to a frenzy. Her mind spun like a Catherine wheel as she felt the soft graze of his stubble on her throat as he kissed her neck so sweetly.

He kissed the way he was himself – slow, tender, thorough, with a hidden force that took over and drove all before it. Rockets screamed across the night sky. Golden flowers burst against her eyelids. And then Alexander made his fatal mistake.

'You're so special,' he murmured.

And then Nikki's mind clicked in, and the first thing it showed her was her mother, clutching at love, refusing to see just how unsuitable her latest young fiancé was, because: 'He makes me feel so special, Nikki, darling. You'll understand when you're older.'

She felt the punch of the memory deep in her heart. How often had she vowed that she would never be ruled by her passions? Part of her protested that Alexander was different, but her panicky mind wouldn't listen. She had planned her defences when she was young and she had promised herself she would stick to them.

She tore herself from his arms.

At once he reached for her to draw her back.

Nikki pushed at his arms. 'I can't. Please let me go!'

He let her go and she ran for the upstairs bathroom.

She locked the door, and looked at her face

in the mirror over the sink. Wide grey eyes stared back. She had never looked better, but there was a tousled wildness about her appearance that scared her. She wanted to be sleek, groomed, and in control.

She snapped on the hot tap and billows of steam filled the room. She reached for her favourite bath soap, scrubbing her hands and face until she smelt like a Nordic pine forest. Then she put gel on her hair and combed it down until it sleeked severely behind her ears. Then, finally, she went back downstairs.

She was aware of her heart thudding uncomfortably as she pushed open the living-room door. Alexander was leaning back against her mantelpiece with his arms crossed, apparently relaxed, but there was a thunderstorm on his face. Her stomach fluttered with butterflies.

'Would you like another cup of coffee?' she asked him.

As he treated her to one of his long silent looks, she felt her cheeks flame.

'I just thought you might like a hot drink before you leave. I think the roads might freeze if you don't set off soon, and that could be dangerous.'

Alexander ignored her babbling and gave a slow smile.

She couldn't meet his eyes.

'It's a long way back and it might not be easy to get a taxi if you don't phone soon.'

He surveyed her for what seemed like a lifetime. Nikki glanced at his face and saw that his eyes were very soft, and very understanding, as he took in her unease and the severity of her hair.

She looked away.

Then her doorbell rang sharply, followed by two bangs on the door.

Alexander beamed at her happily.

'My taxi,' he explained. 'I called for one while you were upstairs.'

Nikki felt awful. She knew she was treating him rudely, but she felt so overwhelmed by the situation that all she could do was send him away.

She watched as he put on his coat. He was so big and warm and comforting. She met the kindness in his eyes and nearly weakened. Surely Alexander was different from the men who had misused her mother?

But wasn't that what Nicole used to say?

'He's different, darling!'

How often had she heard that? From Marie, from her mother, and from every other weak women whose good judgement had left her because of desire. Nikki's resolve hardened. She would have her say.

However, she couldn't look at his face, or meet his eyes, as she spoke.

'This was just a chemistry thing, you know that, don't you? I don't want it to get in the way of work or anything. It was a one-off.'

Alexander reached out and cupped her chin in one hand, tipping it up and forcing her to look at him. The confidence she saw in his eyes was unnerving, but he only said gently, 'Whatever you like, Nikki, darling.'

And then he left her.

9

Alexander To The Rescue

On the way to work the next day, Nikki had to pull off the road to calm herself. She parked in a lay-by on top of a hill that over-looked the moors.

Feeling restless, she jumped out of the car. The rolling moors stretched out under a grey November sky that shimmered like a pearl. Fir plantations were black ebony on the horizon. A bird hovered in the air. Nikki watched it absently for a few minutes, listening to the silence, feeling the cold wind chill her face. She didn't know what kind of bird it was, but she bet Alexander would.

Alexander! She hadn't been able to stop thinking about him since he'd left last night. She'd slept even more badly than usual, unable to escape the sick and uneasy sensations in her chest and stomach.

Her head was still convinced that she'd done the only sensible thing, her heart wasn't so sure. If only the man had protested, become angry over the way she'd dismissed him. If he'd been rude and demanding she'd have seen his true colours and felt justified in her actions.

But he'd been so calm, so gentle and understanding. Men didn't behave like that, did they? They hung around and made demands. But Alexander wasn't like that, was he?

Nikki shivered and got back into the car, and turned on the engine. It was too cold to mope around outside, and whatever Alexander's motives might be, she would have to face him sometime so it might as well be now.

Linda was waiting for her on the factory steps.

'Not another crisis?' Nikki asked anxiously.

Linda shook her head vigorously.

'Alexander asked me to wait for you,' she explained. 'He said you'd be arriving round about now. He's called a meeting in the canteen. There were so many rumours flying around that he thought it best to get the true situation out in the open.'

Nikki followed Linda along the echoing corridors. They pushed open the big swing doors of the canteen and she saw Alexander himself at the head of the room.

He had never looked bigger or more handsome.

She felt the breath catch in her throat and her heart vibrated in her chest. It took a colossal effort of will to meet his gaze. But why on earth was he holding an immense stainless steel teapot?

She forgot all her shyness and stared at him outright, finding nothing in his eyes but friendly good humour.

'Are you going to risk a cup? I brewed it myself.'

'He makes a good cuppa,' vouched several of the staff.

Nikki took her cup of tea in silence. She was used to talking. She always talked – to keep things moving, to win people over, to ease an awkward silence. But now, faced with Alexander making tea for the whole factory, she simply didn't know what to say.

Linda was watching her with concern.

'Are you OK, Nikki, love? You're terribly pale.'

She couldn't pretend she was one hundred per cent.

'Don't come too close!' she said. 'I think I'm fighting off some kind of bug.'

Her secretary just laughed and ushered her to a chair.

'Sit down next to me and don't worry!' Linda told her. 'I've had lots of practice with my daughter Chloe's school bugs. They bite me and die.'

Nikki felt better once she was seated. The tea was good, as promised; hot and refreshing. She felt her troubled stomach ease as she sipped it. She'd survived the first encounter with Alexander, and it was curiously comforting to have Linda by her side.

Then she forgot her own concerns as Alexander opened the meeting.

He was as different from Norman Thompson as it was possible to be.

Nikki craned her head and scanned the room but the manager hadn't come to the meeting. Just as well. The old man would have had a fit if he could have heard Alexander laying out the whole truth, simply and eloquently, to the assembled workers.

He spread both his hands wide and looked around as he finished.

'So you see, we are living on borrowed time. If we don't get the prototypes finished in time for the Harrogate Baby Carriage Fair, and if the buyers don't place some lucrative orders, the receiver will close down the factory for ever.'

Nikki shuddered under the weight of the hostile glares she was receiving, and she heard several uncomplimentary mutters.

One big man had the courage to shout out loud what everyone else was whispering under their breath. His words weren't nice.

'Nikki could have closed this place down two weeks ago!' Alexander roared back at him. 'She's put her job on the line to give us a chance! She has the power to close us down this very second if she wants to, but she's agreed to give us a chance. Anyone want to argue with that? Still want to call her names?'

'No. Sorry.'

The worker turned to Nikki. She was aware of the hush in the room as every factory hand in the place craned closer to hear what was said.

'I'm sorry, Miss Marlow. I didn't know how things stood.'

She nodded, glad that the storm was blowing over.

'Apology accepted.'

'Is it true that your job's on the line?' he asked her.

His expression was earnest.

She couldn't fight the surge of worry the question produced in her. She knew that her voice would shake if she tried to be serious, so she kept it light.

'Only if we fail.'

The assembled workers seemed to read the truth more from her demeanour than from her words.

She found herself explaining in a low, clear voice.

'It's true that I wanted to close the place down at first. When I saw how run-down the factory was, I didn't think there was any hope. But Alexander convinced me to give the place a chance. It's up to you now. It costs a lot of money to keep this factory open, but I'll let it keep going until the Harrogate show. If you can make Davidson's Baby Carriage Company a success again, no-one will be happier than me.'

Her words surprised even herself. Since when had she wanted to save the factory? But she didn't have time to examine her change of heart. The man who'd been swearing at her only a few minutes earlier grabbed both of her hands.

'I'm right sorry I swore at a little lass like you. I didn't know how it was.'

Nikki met the man's eyes. 'Don't look so worried!' she said. 'I've been known to use a few less than polite words myself on occasion.'

His eyes swept over her dainty appearance and Nikki could see that he didn't believe her.

Alexander, however, was standing behind him and his eyes were alight with amusement. He knew she could be fierce, all right! He tipped her a mischievous wink before turning to the staff.

'Back to it, everyone!' he roared. 'There's a lot of work to get through before we can reach the happy ending.'

As the workers filed out, he turned to Nikki, still with that smile in his eyes. A zing of pure pleasure zoomed through her.

She saw a tinge of embarrassment staining his cheekbones and her heart lurched. Was he remembering how they'd kissed?

'Nikki, I didn't forget what you said, about wanting to fight your own battles, but I didn't stop to think. He made me so angry.'

So, he wasn't thinking about their intimacy at all. She had never known anything like the hurricane of emotions that blasted through her.

Suddenly she hated him for being able to upset her so. She raised her head and looked at him coolly.

'Yes, well, let's not have any more primitive frenzies of any kind. It's so bad for business.'

The flush on his cheekbones deepened and she knew that he had understood her double meaning.

She met his gaze and her breath caught in her throat.

Sunlight from the windows turned his irises from brown to an amber that was almost gold. His expression was clear, honest, and wounded.

Her heart moved in her chest as she realised that she had the power to hurt him. She wanted to undo her words at once, but he was already turning away.

'I agree,' he said. 'Let's concentrate on work.'

The moment was gone. And it was probably for the best.

Nikki sighed and made her way to her office with a heavy heart.

Over the next few weeks she threw herself into her work, arriving early and often leaving very late, and all that time Alexander was never less than the gentleman. He didn't make a move towards her. His control was perfect. He never, by word, hint or expression, so much as suggested that there had ever been any intimacy between them.

It drove her crazy.

Nikki's insomnia returned in full force, but she didn't go clubbing. She lay awake at night, staring at the ceiling, trying to fathom Alexander out.

Working with him revealed a lot about his character and she was increasingly coming to understand him. Yes, he saw the world differently from her, but she had to admit that she respected him. She was beginning to see how, without ever compromising the factory's best interests, he strove to produce the best outcome in every situation for all concerned.

If only she hadn't been haunted by dreams of his kisses. She lay awake, staring at the ceiling with burning eyes.

The next morning, she staggered out of bed and into the shower feeling awful from lack of sleep. No man was worth this mental turmoil. She had her life. She was free. She was independent. A partnership at Bosworth's would give her everything she wanted.

She snapped off the hot water and threw on her clothes. The partnership was within her grasp – she mustn't give into mental weakness now.

Incredibly, she was beginning to think they stood a good chance of saving the factory, because the new buggy designs were fantastic. Even Norman Thompson had begun to agree that they were good. The combination of outdoor technology and lightweight design was showstopping. The focus groups reported nothing but enthusiasm.

Nikki was full of optimism as she drove over the late November moors towards the factory.

Soon after she got there, she stood smoothing a dark green fabric between her fingers and said to Linda, 'This is for the Ascot range, right?'

'That's right,' confirmed her secretary. 'Waterproof dark green for the outer skin, teamed with the bamboo and panda design for the inner fabrics.'

Nikki surveyed the panda design doubtfully.

'Isn't it a bit twee?'

'No way!' Linda protested. 'It's so cute I could eat it. And have you seen the navy blue swatches yet? The design team have come up with some lovely little polar bears. I could fetch the swatches from Alan's office if you'd like to see them.'

As Linda bustled off to find the samples, Nikki commented to Alexander – who was in her office checking some figures – that Linda seemed very enthusiastic about the pram linings.

'She seems very enthusiastic about Alan Marsh, too,' confided Alexander. 'I suspect we'll soon be hearing wedding bells from their direction and – hopefully – the patter of tiny feet not too long after. Linda's a marvellous mother. She's really struggled to bring up her little girl on her own since her husband died, and a good job she's made of it. I'm sure she and Alan will be keen to start a family of their own.'

'Well, good luck to her, if that's what she wants, but I don't want to lose the best secretary I ever had!'

'Isn't it rather old fashioned to assume she won't carry on working?'

'If she has any sense,' said Nikki with a snort of derision, 'she'll insist on staying at home. Being a working mother is a massive con trick! The woman just ends up doing two jobs.'

In the long silence that followed, she wondered if she had been too strident.

'After all,' she added hastily, 'there are responsibilities involved in marriage and having children. It's not always wise to try to hold down a job as well.'

'Well, yes,' he agreed. 'You can't do an eighty-hour week if you have children, I'll admit. But Linda will still be relatively young when her children are grown up and she'll be ready to get on with her career.'

'She won't go far. She'll never break through the glass ceiling, not if she takes a career break. Women have to work twice as hard to get to the top.'

Alexander nodded gravely. 'True. And have you ever wondered what waits for you above that glass ceiling?'

'I'll tell you when I get there.'

He shook his dark head decisively.

'There is no there when you get there,' he said quietly. 'Did no-one ever tell you that? You'll push and you'll hustle and if your health holds out you might make it to the top, but what then, Nikki? You'll be alone and scared of a lonely retirement so you'll start fighting all your younger colleagues who are after your job because you'll be desperate to keep working until you drop. Anything to keep you busy enough so that you don't have to admit that you've never really engaged with life, or the people around you.'

She stared at him and he stared back at her.

'Being alone isn't so bad,' she retorted.

'I hope you won't be lonely on your death-bed, Nikki.'

His vehemence was scaring her. She looked away.

'I'll be too busy dying to notice.'

He refused to join in with her lighter tone.

'You'll know, Nikki. No matter how ill you are, you'll know if there's someone in the room who cares for you.'

Startled, she glanced back at him. The emotion that filled her heart was so raw that she could hardly breathe for a second. She remembered her mother as she'd last seen her, tucked tightly into a tidy single bed. She never moved, she never responded. Only the rise and fall of the sheet told you that she was alive.

Could Alexander be right? If so, she was a terrible daughter, because it was more than she could do to visit.

'Don't ladle that hippy dippy new age stuff

over my head,' she snapped.

Alexander looked startled.

A lump caught in her throat, and a small and traitorous voice whispered that she only had to fling herself at him and he would catch her and make her feel better. But she couldn't do it.

He was still watching her closely and Nikki turned away, thinking that as soon as she felt a bit stronger, she would make the long drive down to North Wales to see her mother. She might even stay a week. The sea air would make her feel better.

'You're doing too much, Nikki. You look awful,' Alexander told her.

'Thank you.'

'You could at least take Sundays off.'

Nikki lifted her chin. 'I'm planning to take a week off as it happens – as soon as the Harrogate show is over.'

There was nothing but gentle concern in his eyes as he said, 'If you haven't made yourself ill by then.'

She was glad when Linda returned with the fabric samples.

Nikki selected and rejected patterns with part of her mind while another part of her continued to think about Alexander – and her reaction to him.

As she went on to the next task, and Alexander went away to supervise the factory floor, she admitted to herself that she missed him if they weren't working together.

Alexander was right about her doing too much. She struggled increasingly as time wore on and she felt so drained by the end of the day that she hardly protested at all when Alexander sauntered into her office on the dot of five, looking very determined.

'Time to go home, Nikki.'

'I just want to finish these loading bills.' Her protest was mechanical.

'You could work until you collapsed and still not get to the end of them. Now, go home! I want you on form for the meeting with the Italian hydraulic connector manufacturers tomorrow. Somehow we have to convince them to let our order jump the queue.'

The next morning, as she drove to the hotel where they were meeting the manufacturers, Nikki knew that she looked lacklustre.

Alexander was already at the hotel having coffee with the Italians in the lobby, and when Nikki took a sip of the black coffee that was offered to her, she shuddered as she swallowed it. The hotel brew was awful. It upset her system so much that it was all she could do to concentrate on the meeting, but somehow she persuaded the Italians to agree to make the hydraulic connecting devices and to deliver them before the headline.

'For so beautiful a woman, we must make-a the miracle!' gushed the chief spokesman.

He had been flirting with her the whole morning, but Nikki felt nothing but indifference for his wonderful good looks. She turned down his invitation to lunch and felt unaccountably depressed when Alexander seemed not to care.

The two of them drove back to the factory in separate cars.

When Nikki arrived there a good ten minutes before him it was to find another message from the nursing home waiting for her on her desk.

'Is Dr Evans there, please? It's Nicole Barton's daughter,' she said, returning the call.

She had forgotten about the argument she'd had with the doctor the last time they'd spoken, but she soon realised that she wasn't forgiven. The doctor's cool tone, when he finally condescended to come to the phone, confirmed it.

'Miss Marlow, I'm so glad that you could

find the time to get in touch.'

Nikki wasn't interested in games.

'How is my mother?' she asked.

'Not too well, I'm afraid. She's suffered another seizure, you see.'

Nikki shuddered as she remembered the terrible series of strokes that had led to her mother's present condition. Her whole being felt twisted up with stress as she listened to the doctor's words.

'She's very poorly. It would be best if you could visit her, don't you think?'

For the first time in more than three years, Nikki seriously considered the idea, but her gaze strayed to the work piled high on her desk.

'I'm sorry, but I'm afraid I can't get away.'

Dr Evans' tone became nasty. 'I'm bound to say that I think it's time to order your priorities, my dear.'

Nikki felt the full irony of the situation. When she'd had plenty of leave owed to her by Bosworth's she'd been able to forget her mother for weeks at a time. But now that Alexander had stirred up her conscience, and she wanted to visit, she really couldn't.

'I'll come when I can,' she said simply.

Nikki put down the phone and opened her personal organiser, wondering what she could cancel – but everything was so urgent! There was so little time and so much to do if the factory were to have any chance at all at the Harrogate show. Her stomach burned, her chest hurt, and she felt a cold sweat break out on her skin.

She rummaged in the drawer of her desk and pulled out her favourite patent indigestion remedy.

Ten minutes later she was wondering why it wasn't working. Instead of subsiding, her indigestion was radiating out into her back.

She felt decidedly unwell as she staggered to her feet.

'I can't go sick,' she muttered to herself. 'I've too much work to do.'

But for Nikki, the rest of the day was torture. The last event in her diary was a full board meeting in the stately mahogany-panelled meeting room, and she was so exhausted that she just wished everyone would go away and let her go home.

Half an hour into the meeting, Nikki noticed that Lord Foulridge was looking at her, a worried expression on his face.

'Nikki, my dear, forgive me for asking, but do you feel quite well?'

In truth she was feeling worse by the

second. Only the protective shell she'd built up over the years was keeping her upright in her seat.

However, she felt a strange sense of shame about her infirmity and the habits of a lifetime made her hide her true feelings.

'I have a headache, that's all. Is there any other business?'

Nikki saw both Hugh Foulridge and Olivia Marsden put away several papers that they had clearly intended to discuss, but she didn't have the strength to challenge them. She would have to take it on trust that the issues involved weren't urgent. She needed all her energy just to stay upright until the room was empty. Then she sat alone on her mahogany chair and fought the urge to rest her head on the gleaming table.

A large hand touched her shoulder.

'Nikki, you really don't look well. Let me drive you home.'

Alexander. He had come back for her. She felt the comfort of his quiet presence radiating from him and touching her like a balm. The urge to lean on him had never been stronger, but still she clung to her independence.

'I'm fine. Like I said, it's just a headache.'

'Can I get you anything from the chemists?'

'No, thanks. I have painkillers in my office.'

She was surprised when he nodded acceptance and left the room.

She sat limply at the table, her mind drifting, hoping he would return, but the boardroom remained empty so she hauled herself to her feet and staggered back to her office.

Linda had gone home and the neatly-typed minutes of the board meeting had been left in the middle of her otherwise empty desk.

Nikki picked up the papers but she felt too ill to read. Her eyes stung. The bright lights were bothering them.

She turned off the fluorescent strip. The dimness was better. A nice soft light from the corridor filtered through the glass at the top of the partition wall. It was soothing, peaceful. Perhaps if she rested quietly for a few moments, she would feel better.

She lowered herself into her chair but she couldn't get comfortable. Her stomach was aching steadily.

She would lie flat on the floor. That sometimes helped her indigestion. At least the floor was clean now.

As she lay on the cold stone floor, she felt oddly hot and then cold.

Her mind started to wander and she wasn't sure if she was awake or dreaming.

She thought she'd gone to find Alexander but he didn't want her and so she fell back, crying in disbelief.

Then she thought she was a child again, wandering the streets, looking for the father who would never return.

Then she dreamed that she had died and was sealed into a stone-cold tomb. At least, she hoped it was a dream, because dying hadn't eased the pain. It still gnawed at her with bright steely teeth. She struggled through layers of fever and opened her eyes. It was cold.

It was dark, but the shapes around her were familiar and she knew that she was in her office at the factory. She must have dozed a little, or maybe a lot.

Nikki came round a bit more and realised that the corridor outside was dark and empty. But if the machines were off then it must be past ten o'clock.

She tried to get to her feet, but when she moved, the ferocity of the pain that knotted in her stomach sent her gasping back to the floor. Nausea swept through her, but she fought it down. Cold sweat slicked her brow. This was no time to be ill. She couldn't afford to be ill. She had to do things, she had to stay in control.

Another blast of pain weakened her physically but sharpened her wits.

With awareness came terror. There was something seriously wrong with her. Her handbag was on her desk and her mobile phone was inside it. She was too far gone now to worry about losing face by calling for help. She must get to a phone and dial for an ambulance.

She struggled to sit up. She would suffocate if she couldn't get more air into her lungs. Her stomach cramped. She felt as if the lining was ripping free of its moorings. She was horrified when she was sick on the office floor. Her weakness was unbelievable.

I'm going to die, she thought in total terror. I'm going to die right here on this cold factory floor because I'm all alone and nobody knows I'm here.

Then the door opened and she sensed a dark shadow in the doorway.

'Nikki?'

The sound of that soft strong voice brought instant relief, followed by agonising pain.

She spoke in a voice as weak and plaintive as a small child's.

'I don't feel well.'

She knew that she was trusting him to accept the burden, and he didn't let her down. His voice was calm and steady and infinitely reassuring.

'Where's the pain, Nikki?'

'Everywhere. But my stomach's the worse. My stomach is on fire.'

Alexander didn't reply, but Nikki heard the pop and buzzing of fluorescent tubes before they sprang into incandescent light.

She closed her eyes against the brightness, but even through her lashes, her world turned crimson. Red on her hands, red on her clothes, a great spreading pool of red on the floor around her. Blood! She heard a soft sound as Alexander registered the sight. Had she ever thought him slow?

He was across the room before she could take another breath. His hand was cool on her burning forehead as he examined her and weighed up the situation.

The pain flared and got worse. It was eating her up.

She was beyond normal communication but she sensed the responsibility for her well-being move out of her hands and into Alexander's, and she was well content to have it there.

She was fighting for her life, but she knew he was on her side, and that he would do whatever was necessary to save her.

10

Nikki Fights For Life

The ambulance ride and her arrival at hospital were never clear in Nikki's memory but she retained fragmented impressions of pain, machines, medical smells, doctors and nurses. Even in her frightened agony, she was aware of all the magic of technology that was being used to save her. But more importantly, she could feel the warm reassurance of Alexander's presence by her side. Nikki knew she wouldn't die while he was with her.

Time passed; consciousness slowly emerged from confusion and eventually Nikki opened her eyes to an empty hospital room.

She blinked. The room – no, not a room, she was in a bed surrounded by drawn curtains – felt all wrong without Alexander. Then curtain rings clattered as a massive hand drew them aside and she was smiling because she felt right again.

His face suffused with a golden glow when he saw her.

'You're awake!'

Her mouth was parched and her lips stuck together as she tried to answer.

'I don't … want this drip … in my arm.'

A nurse in white trousers whisked around the screens.

'Could we manage a little drink now? We need plenty of liquids if we're to get better.'

Nikki drank and then slept.

When she woke again, the nurse was gone, but Alexander sat on a hard chair beside her bed, holding her hand.

She slept a lot, slipping in and out of consciousness in a way that wasn't unpleasant. But she always felt better when Alexander was there. He seemed to radiate calm and peace.

Once the uncomfortable tube in the back of her hand had been taken out then she knew she was getting better.

The next day she felt well enough to ask a question that had been troubling her.

'The factory? How are they managing without us?'

Alexander's eyes were calm.

'Everyone knows what to do.'

Nikki drifted off to sleep again. For some

reason, she dreamt about her mother off and on all through that night, but she woke up feeling so much better, quite well enough to confront the medical team that surrounded her bed during the morning ward round.

'When can I go home?'

Dr Yunnis looked at her with his melting black eyes.

'My dear young lady! You have been sick enough to occupy a National Health bed for five whole days! What does that tell you?'

'Five days!' exclaimed Nikki.

The doctor turned to the white-coated figures around him.

'Who can tell me of the warning signs for peptic ulcers?'

Nikki now noticed how young the faces above the white coats were, and realised that she was surrounded by medical students. An earnest young female spoke up eagerly.

'Loss of appetite and steady weight loss.'

'Good!' said the doctor, fixing his gaze on a spotty young man. 'And what sensations can we expect the patient to complain of?'

'Burning in the upper abdomen, radiating into the back and chest.'

'Excellent,' said Dr Yunnis. He turned to Nikki.

'Can you enlighten my students as to why

such an obviously sensible young lady such as yourself should ignore such distressing symptoms?'

Nikki felt like all kinds of fool as she muttered, 'I thought it was indigestion.'

As the doctor turned back to his students and regaled them with gruesome symptoms, Nikki wished that she'd had a more romantic kind of illness. But at least she knew now what was wrong with her. She put her hand on the spot on her chest that had burned so often.

'Are you saying that I have ulcers?'

Doctor Yunnis smiled kindly.

'Hopefully not any more. You have had triple therapy, young lady. We've knocked them out with two strong antibiotics and a powerful bismuth.'

He turned back to his students. 'The young lady should now eat soup, cabbage juice, fish, chicken, well-cooked vegetables and diluted fruit juices. Also, she should learn to meditate.'

Nikki struggled up on her pillows.

'Do what?'

Doctor Yunnis smiled down at her with his panda-dark eyes.

'You must learn to relax.'

'Can't I have pills instead?'

'If you wish. But your husband is quite right in suggesting that your malady may recur if you do not change the lifestyle that caused you to fall ill.'

Husband! thought Nikki, but given Alexander's proprietorial way, the mistake was a natural one. And it could work to her advantage.

'Can I go home?'

The doctor shook his head firmly.

'Not for another forty-eight hours. I want you here in hospital in case the bleeding starts again.'

Nikki felt weary beyond belief. She was sick of the smells and noises of hospital. She wanted privacy and her life back.

A few days later she felt great. When Dr Yunnis poked his head around the screens she announced cheerfully, 'I'm cured!'

The doctor's dark eyes held a warning.

'Do you understand how ill you have been?'

Nikki nodded vehemently.

'I'll be sensible if you let me go home.'

'I'll talk to your husband about it. I will only allow your discharge if he promises to look after you.'

So the hospital still seemed to be under the misapprehension that Alexander was her husband. Nikki said nothing to put them right, and she noticed with some amusement that Alexander also let pass several opportunities to correct them.

She waited until she was snugly ensconced in a taxi before commenting, 'That was a lucky mistake! They'd never had let me leave if they'd known I was going home alone.'

The taxi pulled away from the hospital. Alexander looked down at her with calm brown eyes.

'You're not.'

'What do you mean?'

'I mean you're coming home with me.'

'With you?' she repeated dumbly.

'Do you want to be alone in the middle of the night if you start feeling ill again?'

'I could hire a nurse,' she murmured weakly.

'You could.'

She glanced up and saw the infinite tenderness in his loving brown eyes. Her protests melted away into the simple truth.

'But I'd rather stay with you.'

He stared at her for a long moment. Nikki saw that he looked taken aback, but he soon started laughing.

'What? No tiger claws today? I thought for sure you'd put up a fight when I kidnapped you.'

'I can't summon up the energy,' she admitted.

His arms went around her in a hug that was infinitely reassuring.

'You'll feel that way for a while. But don't worry. I'll look after you.'

Nikki let herself sink into the warmth of his chest. His fleece sweater was as cuddly as she'd always thought it would be. His arms went around her and she sank peacefully into them. She felt deliciously comfortable.

And as she drifted off to sleep she realised that she wouldn't have exchanged the comfort of Alexander's arms for a lottery win.

11

A Homecoming

Nikki woke as the taxi slowed down and the wheels crunched over gravel. She blinked sleepily at the honey-coloured stone mansion before them.

'Is this your house?'

Alexander opened his door to get out, leaving her alone on the back seat. Cold air that smelt of the country rushed into the car.

Nikki shivered and tried to pull herself up. Her legs trembled and she fell back on the seat with a sigh of frustration. Her weakness infuriated her. Alexander leaned in through the back door of the taxi.

'Can't you wait two seconds while I pay the driver?' he grumbled.

'I can do it.'

He stood back and regarded her with sardonic eyes.

'Fine.'

Nikki managed to swing her legs out so that they hung over the side of the car seat and touched the ground, but that was as much as she could manage. Alexander stepped forward and lifted her and Nikki savoured the sensation of being so easily gathered up and carried in a man's arms.

Then she noticed the grandness of the entrance hall.

'I feel like Scarlett O'Hara!'

A sensible Yorkshire housekeeper bustled forward and spoke sharply.

'Don't keep her out in the cold, Alexander. Get her inside, quick!'

Nikki turned her head to smile at the woman and looked directly into button-black eyes.

The housekeeper did a double-take and looked at Nikki more closely.

'My word! There's nowt to her! I'll have my work cut out to feed her up.'

'The hospital have sent a diet sheet, Beryl. We need to take care with what we feed her,' Alexander said as he crossed the black and white hall and carried Nikki up the sweep of the stairs.

Beryl bustled after them and then led the way down the corridor. She came to a halt and flung open a door.

'Get yourself into that bed at once,' she ordered Nikki. 'I'll be back in two minutes with some soup.'

Nikki drank her soup – she wouldn't have dared not to – but she went off to sleep immediately afterwards, retaining only a vague impression of the white sheets and Chinese wallpaper that surrounded her.

It wasn't until she next woke up that she properly took in her fabulous surroundings.

The room was the largest she'd ever slept in. The cherrywood sleigh bed was gorgeous. A soft lamp had been left burning on the bedside table and lavish brocade curtains that pooled on to the polished floor were now pulled across the windows.

Nikki snuggled into crisp cotton bedding

and touched the silk covered comforter. As she'd suspected, it was filled with the softest of down. She felt like a fairy-tale princess.

She swung her legs over the side of the bed and pattered towards the ensuite bathroom across the soft rugs that covered most of the gleaming floor, but by the time she'd washed her hands and face in the grand marble washbasin, she was exhausted.

She was less than halfway across the room on her way back to bed when her door opened and Alexander appeared. He was by her side in a second and she was glad to lean on the support of his arm.

He quickly smoothed out the sheet and plumped up the pillows before assisting her back into bed. He tucked the duvet around her and smiled at her with warm brown eyes before replying.

'It won't be long before you're a speed freak again.'

'Am I so awful?'

'Go back to sleep, Nikki. I'm not bantering with you at this time of night.'

Nikki watched him as he padded silently out of the room and closed the door in his unhurried way.

She turned on her pillow and was asleep in seconds.

But in the small hours of the morning she awoke; her stomach was hurting, her head was thumping and she felt hot and disorientated. Fear built in her. Was she going to be ill and alone again? Then she saw Alexander sitting in a large chair by the lamp, rustling the pages of a newspaper. She wanted to call to him but her mouth was so dry that her lips stuck together. As she struggled to moisten them, he looked up and she felt completely safe as their eyes met.

'A drink?' he suggested, throwing down the paper and getting to his feet.

The glass that he held out to her contained cool, perfect magic, but she couldn't drink much. She touched her aching temples with a fingertip. Alexander noticed at once.

'Headache?'

She nodded and he reached out with gentle hands.

'Close your eyes.'

He touched her hot face with exquisite tenderness. His fingers moved lightly over her hairline and then her temples. A peaceful coolness spread through her head. Her headache vanished. He'd charmed it away.

The magic was still with her when she woke the next morning, feeling too contented to move. She snuggled down in the pillows. She could smell toast and coffee, and hear the soft sounds of a distant radio.

She had the wonderful sensation that someone else was looking after things and all was right with the world. Then the door opened and Alexander sauntered in, carrying a tray.

She sat up and smiled at him as he deposited the tray on her knees.

Then she looked down at a glass of plain water in disbelief.

'Didn't I smell coffee?'

'Do you know what coffee does to sensitive stomachs?'

Nikki pulled a face at him, then she picked up a silver spoon and gingerly stirred the contents of a fine old Minton china soup bowl.

She'd never had soup for breakfast before, but it was delicious. She licked her lips thoughtfully. 'Potatoes, herbs, and maybe a touch of lemon?'

'You might be right, but Beryl will never give up her secret recipe.'

Nikki finished her soup.

'Right, I'm getting up now,' she announced.

She grinned at him cheekily and threw back the white sheets, swinging her legs over the edge of the mattress. Her knees began to shake as soon as her bare feet touched the smooth wooden floor. She forced herself to stand up anyway, but the effort made sweat dew her forehead.

The blast of his furious roar nearly knocked her off her feet.

'Get back into bed, you crazy woman! Don't you know that you nearly died!'

A flurry of movement and Nikki was suddenly back in bed, with the covers tucked in around her. She lay back on the pillows and stared up at the enraged man who was looming over her.

'Merciful heavens, woman! Do you think I'll ever forget standing by your bed and seeing the doctors shaking their heads? And what makes me so furious is that you did it to yourself. You made yourself ill by neglecting your body and driving yourself until you dropped! Now you're at it again! How much of a hint do you need? If you don't change your ways you might as lie down on the railway tracks or jump off a high building.'

Nikki could feel the fight draining away from her.

'OK. If it makes you happy then I'll rest, today.'

Their eyes met for a long, slow moment,

then Alexander nodded.

Nikki was asleep seconds later.

She woke up for regular soup meals, and she woke up once in the dark. She didn't know what time it was, but the light went on almost immediately and Alexander padded over to the bed with a glass of water.

Nikki let the cool liquid flow down her throat and handed the empty glass back with a sigh.

'Thank you,' she murmured.

She felt much better the next morning. She was awoken once more by the smell of toast and coffee but this time she didn't argue when Alexander brought in a breakfast tray that contained only a glass of water to drink, because the soup was velvet perfection.

'Beryl should write a soup book,' said Nikki, putting down her spoon with a contented sigh. 'I hardly miss real food at all.'

'That's good, because you're not having any for a while yet.'

'Bully!' she snapped back.

But it was only force of habit that made her retaliate. She didn't feel fractious at all, until Alexander refused to let her wash her hair.

'It's disgusting! It still smells of hospitals. *Please* let me wash it.'

Nikki watched his strong face while he thought it over.

'In a week's time.'

'Tomorrow.'

The shake of his head told her she would get nowhere.

'The day after tomorrow?'

'No, but you can have a visitor for a few minutes on Wednesday.'

'Who would want to come and visit me?'

With a smile in his eyes, Alexander waved a hand at a pile of cards that lay beneath a vase generously filled with perfumed lilies.

'Those people. Who would you like to see first? Linda?'

'You don't know much about women if you think I'll want to see anyone before I've washed my hair.'

'You can wash your hair on Wednesday.'

So Nikki spent the rest of the day opening her get well cards and surreptitiously measuring the distance to the bathroom.

The next day, she picked a moment when she knew Alexander was out, and showered and shampooed until she almost washed herself away.

The very second that he opened the door that evening his gaze went directly to her clean and shiny hair. She waited guiltily, watching angry expressions flit across his face, and was relieved when he merely shook his head in his slow way.

'I feel loads better, Alexander. How's the valuation coming along?'

'I'm not talking about work to you until the New Year.'

'You've got to be kidding me!'

He walked over and settled himself in the chair next to her bed.

She gave him a brilliant smile, and his look of a man being ready to do battle faded at once. He reached out as if he couldn't help himself and touched a strand of her clean, silky hair.

'The doctors have signed you off work until the fifth of January. I mailed the sick note to Bosworth's when I reported your illness.'

She hadn't given her employers a thought.

'Thank you,' she murmured humbly.

At her soft tone he looked up and there was hope in his eyes.

Then Beryl came in with a tray and Alexander got to his feet to take it from her.

'What's the soup recipe this time, Beryl?' he teased.

'You should know better than to ask!'

The housekeeper tossed her head. Her lips were set, but Nikki could see from the pleased glow in the button-black eyes that the woman enjoyed being teased.

Alexander left, and Nikki ate her soup.

As she finished her meal she heard a vacuum cleaner buzzing on the stairs and she wondered how many people worked in the house. It was a huge place to keep clean. Surely Alexander would never have bought such a place as a bachelor pad? She had assumed it was his family home, but if so, where were the rest of the family?

When Beryl came in for the tray, Nikki asked her.

'Well now, this house belonged to the major – Alexander's father. He died many a year ago and Alexander's mother, Patricia, has lived abroad ever since. She went straight back to Egypt after the funeral. Albert's funeral, that is.'

'Egypt?'

Beryl looked disapproving. Her lips nearly vanished. 'She studies tombs and that,' she told Nikki. 'Poking around in burial sites in China and Egypt.'

Nikki looked at the exquisite wallpaper with its pattern of cherry blossom and blue-birds.

'Did she bring this paper back from China? It's so beautiful.'

'Lord, bless you, no. Agnes, the major's mother, fetched that back many years ago. Someone should write a book about that woman. Went off all over the world, she did. China, Africa, one of them icy places with Eskimos in it. The whole family's the same. Alexander's sister, Patty, could easily have found a nice job in England but no, she had to swan off to California. I warned her she'd end up marrying an American and she did.'

'Are there any more brothers and sisters?'

'No. Patricia, she said two children was enough. She wanted to study. I can't see what she wanted another degree for. She already had two of the blessed things. But she said she wouldn't be taken seriously as an archaeologist if she wasn't a professor. We used to joke that she wanted three degrees but only two children. She only took six years off when they were little. Then she went back to work. Not that she needed to work, mind you, but she wanted to.'

'So Alexander's father, the major, was Albert's brother?'

'That's right. Albert didn't marry or have any kids. That's why the factory went to Alexander.'

As Beryl left, Nikki cuddled up again into the crisp white pillows and she realised that she envied Alexander's family. They sounded such interesting people. They travelled the world. They had worthwhile careers and they treasured their family home.

A dim and distant sadness for all she'd missed swept over her, but the past was gone, and she realised that she was close to making peace with it in her heart.

The future was what mattered now, and the urge to get on and build something worthwhile gripped her with full force.

'No!' said Alexander, crossing his arms over his chest and looking down at her.

She tried to look winsome.

'Oh, please. What harm can it do me to just take an insy-winsy, teeny-weeny little look at how the valuation papers are progressing?'

'Absolutely not.'

She glared back at him.

'Well, can I see the report later in the week?'

'No.'

'A week on Monday?'

This time he paused and considered her suggestion.

'Please, please, *please*, Alexander,' she pleaded. 'I need to know what's going on. It'll make me feel better, I promise.'

She could see in his eyes that she'd won,

but there was a warning in his serious tone. 'Only if you continue to improve,' he told her.

Nikki snuggled up under her duvet. 'I'm much, much better,' she told him.

Alexander shook his head.

'On the contrary, you're still very weak. I was thinking about letting you have the papers sooner. You gave in too easily.'

She sat bolt upright and reached for a pillow. She was quite a good shot, but although he didn't seem to be moving quickly, Alexander managed to get through the door and shut it behind him before she could get him. The pillow hit the door and flopped harmlessly to the floor.

'Wretched man!' she growled.

12

Meeting The Family

'Wretched, wretched, man!' she growled again as her visitors started to arrive. Nikki was impatient for news from the factory but Alexander had briefed people thoroughly.

Other than assurances that all was going well, every single person who came to see her refused to talk business with her.

But Nikki was surprised and touched that so many people did call. Her elderly neighbour, Mr Hartley, came to visit, bringing with him her cleaning lady, Marlene, and a much needed suitcase of clothes.

However, although they'd all signed a card for her, no-one from Bosworth's telephoned her or came to visit, despite the fact she had worked there for nearly seven years.

In contrast, she'd only been at Davidson's for a few weeks and had spent most of her time there arguing with people, but they still all came to see how she was.

Lord Foulridge and Olivia Marsden came, together and separately, bringing her baskets of fruit, flowers and the latest novels.

Alan Marsh came, and so did Norman Thompson – who puffed in, bearing an exquisite bunch of dahlias that he shyly confessed he'd grown himself.

'I'm going to concentrate on the garden when I retire,' he told her gruffly, a sad look in his faded eyes. 'I'm beginning to think it might be a good thing. The world's moving too fast for an old codger like me.'

Nikki was suddenly glad beyond belief that

Alexander hadn't allowed her to humiliate the old man in his last few months.

Even some of the factory workers popped in to see her, the bearded trade union official amongst others. He brought a lot of very dull booklets elaborating on sick-pay, but Nikki recognised the very real kindness of his intent, and was grateful.

But the visitor she enjoyed most was Linda. Her secretary visited often, usually alone, but one day she brought her daughter with her.

'Chloe was so brave about having a tooth filled this morning that I've let her have the rest of the day off school.'

'I like school, but visiting you is nice, too,' explained Chloe.

Nikki gazed at Linda's daughter and the self-possessed young lady stared back. She was five years old, remembered Nikki, who was completely unused to children and had no idea what to say. Luckily Chloe wasn't shy. She climbed up on to the bed and snuggled in next to her in the sweetest way.

'I've brought you a card,' she confided, reaching into her cute little pink handbag.

'I've still got the first one you made for me,' Nikki told her, pointing to the bedside table.

Chloe looked up at her with the sparkling

clear eyes of the very young.

'This one's even betterer than that. Me and Mummy made some letters on the computer. Look, it says GET WELL NIKKI! And I put lots of kisses on it.'

'Thank you, darling,' said Nikki.

She dropped a kiss on top of the small head. Chloe's hair smelt deliciously of baby shampoo. The little girl smiled up at her, but the child couldn't help being distracted by the magnificence of the room.

'There are birds all over the wallpaper. Please can I look at them?'

'Look, but don't touch,' warned Linda as Chloe wriggled away.

'She's so lovely,' said Nikki.

Linda's expression softened.

'She's pretty good for her age. It's not been easy, with being on my own since Joe died, but maybe when I'm married to Alan...'

How did Alexander manage to be right every single time?

Nikki sat upright in bed and made herself look surprised.

'Oh, wow! You and Alan?'

Linda looked down and blushed so hard that her neck went crimson.

'I'm so pleased for you,' said Nikki, genuinely delighted.

Linda smiled back at her.

'I never expected to be so happy,' she said.

The blissful expression on her face gave her simple words a force that could not be denied.

Nikki found it easy to initiate a warm hug. 'When's the wedding?'

Chloe danced over. 'Mummy's getting married next summer! I'm going to be a bridesmaid in a new dress,' she said, giggling.

'Are you having a honeymoon?' Nikki asked Linda.

The radiance in Linda's face dimmed as if a rain cloud had dampened it.

'I don't know. We daren't book anything yet. We might not have jobs in the New Year. It's going to be tight for money if we're both out of work.'

Nikki's hands plucked restlessly at the white sheet.

'I wish I could get back to the factory...'

But however much she pleaded, Alexander wouldn't hear of her going back to the factory – or back to her own house – until after Christmas.

Nikki was in the beautifully cosy Edwardian orangery that ran along the south side of Alexander's house when she suggested to him that she should return to her own home.

Through the sparkling glass windows she could see grey December rain falling steadily, but it was warm amongst the bitter-sweet citrus trees with their glossy green leaves and perfumed white flowers.

Alexander leaned forward in his cane chair.

'Please, don't go. Beryl likes cooking for you, and the family will be here soon. They're looking forward to meeting you. It's up to you, sweetheart, but I wish you'd stay.'

As soon as he took the pressure off, Nikki capitulated.

'Well, if you don't mind...'

Now that she was so much better, Alexander was going regularly to both factories during the day, but he steadfastly refused to talk shop when he came home – and Nikki was astonished to find that she hardly cared. She was enjoying the pleasures of occupying the warm cocoon of a sofa in the conservatory with the ever-faithful Beryl to wait on her, and every comfort to hand.

The next evening, Nikki wasn't very hungry and Alexander looked at her with concern as she picked at her food.

'Lovely red, watery eyes,' he observed. 'Bed for you, young lady.'

'I've had my illness quota for a decade. I

can't be getting a cold as well,' she grumbled.

She slept badly that night and was miserable the next morning with a stuffy head. Alexander insisted on staying with her all day. He moved a table and a phone into the conservatory and worked from home.

The attention was overwhelming and Nikki didn't feel that she deserved so much care.

'It's only a cold.'

'And it's only work. I can do it anywhere.' His gaze was long and level.

Nikki blew her red nose and reflected that she seemed to be suffering from a glut of unglamorous ailments. But she felt really low, so she didn't protest when Alexander brought her a cold remedy – one of Beryl's recipes, of course – with herbs and fresh ginger in it. She drank it down and went to sleep on the sofa and didn't wake until bed time.

She felt much better the next day which was just as well because Alexander's sister Patty, her husband Bradley, and Aden and Petrona, their very sophisticated young children, all arrived from California.

'A real family Christmas in Yorkshire!' exclaimed Patty. 'You don't know how much I've been looking forward to this.'

Nikki noticed Patty's tanned American

husband looking longingly at the central heating thermostat.

'Sure is cold in this country,' he observed wryly, but he wrapped a loving arm around his wife as he said it.

'Let's go shopping!' Patty suggested to him. 'I'll buy you some real English sweaters.'

'Well, don't go crazy, honey. There won't be much call for them back home!'

Patty turned to Nikki and spoke spiritedly.

'Do you know how many days of the year are cold and foggy in San Francisco? Brad thinks this is heresy, but the wonderful Californian climate is a myth.'

Patty had the same dark hair and brown eyes as Alexander, but there the resemblance ended. She was thin and wiry and quick as a whip. She was also incredibly friendly.

'Would you be up to going shopping with me, Nikki? It would be much more fun if we could go together.'

'I'd love to!' exclaimed Nikki, who'd just realised that she'd need to buy Christmas presents for everyone.

Alexander looked stern. 'Don't tire yourself out!' he warned.

A teasing sparkle lit Patty's brown eyes as she prepared to cheek her older brother.

'Have you never heard of retail therapy?'

she asked him.

Nikki was astonished to see the Christmas rush in full swing in the shopping mall. It emphasised how much time had passed while she'd been ill. Part of her began to worry about how the factory was getting on, but then the Christmas excitement took over and she started to enjoy herself.

Carols played as she followed Patty around the brilliantly decorated stores. Gaily-wrapped parcels began to pile up in her arms, but Patty didn't let her go on for too long.

'I'm coming back tomorrow with the kids, so if you've forgotten anything I can get it for you,' she promised. 'But I want to get back now, in case Mummy is home. She said to expect her when we see her, but you know what planes from Egypt are like.'

At this reminder of the gulf in their lifestyles, Nikki found it an effort not to fall quiet on the way home. She was dreading meeting Alexander's mother. She thought a professor of Egyptology must be rather forbidding.

Her stomach was in knots by the time they drew up on the gravel sweep outside the house, but Patty dragged her into the kitchen where all was noise and confusion.

Nikki hung back, shyly watching the joyful family reunion, but it was only a few minutes before Alexander's mother enveloped her in a warm hug.

'My poor child! What a time you've been having. We'll all have coffee in the conservatory – I hear it's your favourite place to sit and you can tell me all about yourself.'

Nikki let herself be shepherded along with the rest of the family, wishing that she were truly one of them instead of just a visitor.

Over the next few days she was allowed to help with decorating the tree and making mince pies, but Alexander had left strict instructions that she was not to overdo things.

On Christmas Eve, trying to vacuum her own bedroom, Patty and the children burst in and wrestled the space-age cylinder cleaner away from her.

'I could easily do a bit of housework,' Nikki complained. 'Now that I'm feeling better it's difficult to sit still all day.'

'Try one of Mummy's books,' suggested Patty. 'That should keep you pinned down for a while.'

Nikki felt her heart sink. She usually spent her days looking at a computer and her eyes were usually too tired for reading in the evenings. Consequently she'd never developed the habit of curling up with a book.

She rather hoped Patty would forget the idea, but no sooner had Nikki snuggled into the warmth of the citrus-scented orangery than little Aden appeared carrying a huge tome.

'Grandma's book – for you.'

'Thank you, darling,' she said, taking it from him and feeling obliged at least to open it.

Four hours later, engrossed in the book, she was startled back to reality by someone shaking her shoulder.

'Nikki, do you want to come to midnight mass tonight?'

Alexander! She felt the warm rush of pleasure that seemed to assail her every time she saw his smiling eyes come close to her.

'Oh, yes, please. I think I'd like to.'

His tone was bossy. 'Then you're to go to bed now,' he instructed.

'You can't tell me what to do! You great big prehistoric bully.'

The laugh in his voice was like a tonic. 'No bed, no midnight outing, you mouthy shrimp. And it's going to be clear and frosty tonight.'

Nikki capitulated. She could see from his eyes that he was adamant, and she wasn't fit enough to win an argument with him.

'OK,' she sighed. 'Alexander, why didn't you tell me how well your mother writes? The descriptions are so clear and vivid. The heat, the fascinating customs. I feel like I've actually been there.'

'Leave the book here,' he commanded. 'I want you to get some sleep.'

Her sleep was light but refreshing.

Beryl woke her at a quarter past eleven with the inevitable bowl of soup. Nikki couldn't help exclaiming out loud as she tasted apples and cinnamon and surely a subtle trace of turkey in the creamy vegetable concoction.

'It tastes like Christmas!'

'That's as maybe,' retorted Beryl, giving nothing away. 'But you'd better wrap up warm tonight, Nikki. The church stove never amounts to much with all that stone.'

Nikki cried out in surprise as she walked out of the front door. Patty and Bradley's hired people-carrier had been transformed. White fairy lights twinkled from the mirrors, windows and dashboard. A selection of fake fur rugs warmed every seat. And best of all, silver bells and wind chimes jingled as they drove.

Brad smiled at Nikki. 'I couldn't quite rustle up a horse-drawn sleigh for you, but the kids did pretty good, don't you think?'

'It's fantastic!'

Nikki stroked her fake fur rug and snuggled closer to Alexander. He responded at once, snaking a possessive arm around her and drawing her to him. She was filled with confusion and excitement as the people-carrier rushed through the narrow lanes. Brad slotted a Christmas song CD into the sound system and the whole family sang along to Jingle Bells and White Christmas.

A sudden rush of happiness melted Nikki's shyness and she found herself able to join in the singing. She was almost sorry when they reached the lovely Dickensian town of Appledale, and Brad parked under a lantern in the cobbled market square.

The church was packed with wholesome-looking country folk and the service was a sincere celebration of the true meaning of Christmas.

Red-berried holly, winter-green ivy, and creamily lovely Christmas roses decorated the pews. Flickering candle flames made the church lovely, and Nikki was touched to her heart.

She was silent as the service ended and they filed out into the frosty churchyard.

The family party stood among the ancient yew trees, cheerfully greeting friends from the neighbourhood.

A bright moon made the silver-frosted grass glitter with light and the shadows in contrast looked very black.

The local people looked cheerfully snug in their brightly-coloured hats and scarves, but the crowd was starting to thin as the attraction of mince pies and sherry at home won out over socialising on such a crisp and decidedly chilly night.

Patricia walked over and put her arm through Nikki's. 'My toes are freezing!' she announced. 'Are you warm enough?'

'I'm fine, thank you.'

'Well, I don't know about you, but I've had enough socialising for now. We'll go visiting on Boxing Day. It's a tradition in the area that everyone keeps open house and I hope you'll come with us. People are dying to meet you properly.'

Nikki sat next to Patricia on the way home. Small Aden had fallen asleep next to her and she savoured the feeling of a warm young body in her arms as she looked out of the car window at the neat lines of the ploughed fields and the well-kept hedges of Yorkshire, all glittering with frost by the light of the moon and stars.

As they swept up the driveway and the people-carrier crunched over the gravel and parked in a triumphant jingle of Christmas bells outside the house, Nikki realised how wonderful the enchanted circle of a happy family could be.

13

A Family Christmas

Nikki lent a hand with the impossible task of getting two excited children off to bed on Christmas Eve. She had never imagined how much fun one could have hanging up Christmas stockings. Her heart was glowing as she kissed each of the children goodnight. This was the kind of family experience she'd always longed for as a child.

She was smiling wistfully as she walked back downstairs and pushed open the door of the gracious family room. The Christmas tree next to the glowing fire and the grand piano by the big windows seemed to symbolise all that she'd missed.

'Shall we have a hot chocolate, Nikki, before we turn in?'

She felt a shock race through her whole body as she saw Alexander, waiting by the tree. She suddenly realised that she was alone with him. She backed towards the door.

'No, thank you. I'll just get off to bed, I think.'

'Wait!'

She stopped dead in her tracks, not quite meeting his eyes. She had time to smell the fir scent of the Christmas tree and listen to the logs crackling in the fireplace while he decided what to say next.

'Come and sit down.' He gestured towards the leather sofa. 'I think we need to talk.'

'No, I don't think so.'

'Then we'll have our discussion standing. What are you so afraid of?'

'I'm not.'

His tone was soft and coaxing. 'Why are you still clinging on to that protective shell?' he asked her.

'It's not a shell, it's the real me. I'm hard and I'm selfish and I think you'd do better to leave me alone.'

His head moved in a slow, slow shake.

'You're not hard, Nikki. You're deter-mined, but you listen. You weren't afraid to change your mind and keep the factory open. And there isn't a selfish bone in your body. No-one could work harder than you.'

She was ridiculously touched by his compliments. She looked at his deep brown eyes, and her voice choked up as she questioned him softly.

'What is it you want?'

He held out both hands in an open, encouraging gesture, but it was a long time before the words came.

'To marry you.'

Nikki felt the shock like an electric thump to her whole body. She hadn't expected a proposal. Her heart was racing and she reeled with the strength of the conflict inside her.

At last she acknowledged the force of her yearning to have a family of her own; a happy, loving family where she belonged.

But along with that awareness came the powerful terror created by her mother's past experiences.

What if she put all her trust in Alexander and he let her down?

She was too frightened to take the chance.

'I can't marry you. I can't give up my independence.'

'Why not think about what you'd be adding to your life?' he asked her.

His eyes were so loving, so persuasive and brown as he held her gaze, searching her eyes deeply the way he often did, and this time he seemed to find what he'd been looking for.

He reached for her gently and put his face next to hers. It felt so good to have it gently resting there, warm male skin against the cold silk of her cheek.

'You're so lovely,' he murmured. The soft words were just a rumble deep in his chest, more a vibration than a sound. 'I'd do anything for you.'

Nikki felt all the security of the house and the family around her, and she felt safe enough to be honest. 'I'm afraid to let myself fall in love,' she admitted.

Alexander sighed.

Suddenly she couldn't stay in his arms any longer. She tore herself away and, refusing to let herself turn again to look at him, ran from the room and pattered up the softly-lit sweep of the staircase.

Her bedroom felt like a refuge.

Sentiment burned in her heart as she saw that a Christmas stocking had been hung at the foot of her bed.

Love overflowed in this family so why was it so difficult to accept it?

She fell asleep resolving to talk with Alexander in the morning. She would tell him a little about her early life so that he would understand. She owed him that much at least.

Long before dawn, Nikki heard the thudding of small feet followed by howls of childish excitement. Deciding that it was only time to get up if you were under ten years old, she drifted off again.

The next time she woke she was still filled with a delicious feeling of languor, but her internal clock told her it was time to get up and as she went down to the kitchen she could smell the delicious aromas of coffee and cinnamon.

The family turned bright faces towards her and chorused a greeting when she walked into the breakfast room.

Alexander lifted a bunch of mistletoe, pulled her to him and kissed her cheek. 'Good morning, gorgeous.'

None of the family seemed to make anything of his kiss, but Nikki felt her face flaming red.

The big family table was scattered with toast racks, cereal bowls, coffee mugs, and big pots of honey and jam. Nikki made her way over to an empty chair next to Patricia but within half a second of sitting down she found herself lifted in the air as Alexander scooped her up and then settled her on to his knee.

'There's only one spare chair,' he told her firmly, 'so you'll just have to share it with me.'

And then he kissed her again.

'How gross! Soppy stuff!' said little Petrona.

Alexander poured himself a coffee and then, after a moment's consideration, poured another cup for Nikki.

'It's allowed today – special Christmas treat,' he told her. Then he looked at his oldest nephew. 'What did you get for Christmas, short stuff?'

Nikki felt breathless and embarrassed, but since there really wasn't another chair, she took a sip of coffee and tried to calm herself.

The coffee was good, Alexander's favourite aromatic blend. She took another sip and began to relax and even to enjoy the experience of sitting on his knee, being fed bites of his toast and marmalade.

After breakfast, the children dragged

everyone over to the tree to open their presents. Nikki sat on the rug in front of the crackling fire and was so glad she'd let the Christmas mood get the better of her when she'd gone shopping. She'd bought everyone terrific presents, which was lucky, because her gifts from the family were not just generous, but so carefully chosen that she felt warmed through her entire being.

Feeling reckless, she drank another cup of coffee and ate a mince pie, thoroughly enjoying the fun of exclaiming over everyone's gifts, until finally Petrona asked, 'Uncle Alex, didn't you buy a present for Nikki?'

Alexander dug in his pocket and produced a small square box wrapped in green paper and tied up with a crushed gold ribbon. He looked down and turned the box over in his hand.

'Yes, I did buy Nikki a present, but she doesn't want it.' His tone was sad.

'What is it?' persisted Aden.

Alexander looked at the bright faces of his young relatives.

'An engagement ring,' he told them honestly.

Brad, who was sprawled full length on one of the leather sofas, lifted his head and drawled languidly to his brother-in-law, 'You mad fool! Take the ring back to the shop and run while you can. You don't know what kind of hell it is, being married.'

Patty fell on him with a cushion, and the children joined in, screaming with joy at this chance to create a little mayhem.

Patricia's eyes were dark, remembering. 'It took me nearly a year to accept your father's proposal,' she told Alexander. 'Even now I sometimes wonder if I should have said no. I was offered the chance to go to Cambodia. The discoveries I could have made ... the books I could have written...'

Patty tired of pummelling her husband and came over to her mother. She was only half teasing, when she asked her, 'Weren't we worth it?'

Patricia's hazel eyes sparkled. She stood up and gave Patty an unselfconscious hug, then rested her cheek lightly against her daughter's.

'Of course you were, darling.'

They held their affectionate position a few seconds longer, the perfect picture of mother and daughter closeness.

Nikki felt her heart twist in her chest and a lump grow in her throat as she watched them. If only she and her mother could have enjoyed such an easy, loving relationship.

To her relief nobody, including Alexander, mentioned his proposal again or tried to pressure her into changing her mind. The family bore her no ill-will for turning him down. She seemed to be welcome just as she was, a fact that soothed and healed a tender spot so deep in her being that she hardly knew it was there.

She'd never spent a better Christmas and New Year.

It was hard to say goodbye to Patricia when she went back to Egypt, and tears were very close as Nikki stood on the honey-coloured stone steps outside the house, waving Patty and her family goodbye.

Alexander was watching as she reached for her handkerchief.

'I'll miss those children,' she explained apologetically.

'We could have some of our own,' he said casually.

Startled, her gaze flew to his face. He hadn't said another word about marriage since Christmas morning.

Nikki realised now that she had been refusing to think about the subject so that it wouldn't spoil the lovely fun of the holiday, and now she was completely unprepared to deal with his comment.

She looked at him helplessly, aware of grey clouds in the sky behind him, the cold air and the frost on the hedges. She saw his expression turn sad, just a fraction, like a light being dimmed. He tucked her arm in his and towed her back into the house.

'Let's not stand out here getting cold. We could wrap up and go for a walk later, if you like.'

The walk was beautiful, in a cold, wintry kind of way. They found holly with red berries and Alexander taught her how to identify jackdaws from their raucous cries of 'chack! chack!' he knew what all the birds were and he could tell her what crops the ploughed ground was being prepared for.

But all the time they walked and talked, Nikki was aware of tension between them. Alexander's throw-away comment had destroyed the harmony that had borne them through Christmas and the New Year.

'We have to talk,' she said at last.

They were crossing the grassy rise of a big field, all silver-green with frost. They walked to the other side of the field without any comment from Alexander until he'd settled her down comfortably on the top rail of a wide wooden stile. He stood before her, leaning forward slightly to examine her face. Nikki knew she could confide in him, but it was difficult to know where to start.

'We're so different,' was all she could think of to say.

He held her face and kissed her cold lips gently before replying, 'Does it matter?'

She felt the light wind tugging at her hair. Birds flew across a sky that was the colour of an oyster shell, gently glowing with all shades of grey.

'It does matter, because–'

Alexander cut her off, speaking in a low and urgent tone. 'I understand more about you than you think, Nikki. Don't say any more now.'

She sighed deeply, and knew that he was being wise. Fragments of her past life still swirled around her, confusing her, making it hard to know what was right. Her heart told her that she was happier than she'd ever been before, but her head was still warning her off. They should wait a while to let things settle. She voiced aloud the only thing she was clear about– 'The holiday is over.'

As he held her close, she rubbed her cold cheek against his warm one and felt safe in his arms.

He drew back and looked at her. 'Let's take it slowly, Nikki.'

She deliberately chose to read his comment as if it was about her health. 'I'm ready to go back to work tomorrow,' she told him.

She saw him consider her remark, then decide to accept her change of subject. She was relieved. Whatever the outcome of their relationship, they had to work together until the fate of the factory was resolved.

'Why not wait until the day of the fair? I'll take you to Harrogate with me on Wednesday.'

She laughed, wanting to lighten the mood. 'But I might as well start from Monday morning. The doctor says I'm fine now, so why can't I go back? What are you hiding down at the factory? You keep telling me it's all going smoothly.'

'It is,' he pronounced with a confident air. 'I promise you it's all going beautifully.'

14

Nikki Saves The Day

Nikki felt as if she'd been away for a whole lifetime as they drove through the big gates of the factory the next morning. She had been through so much that it was a surprise to see the factory looking just the same.

'Nothing's changed,' she remarked in wonder as they crossed the cobbled yard to the stone entrance.

Alexander gave her a glance that she found unreadable, but he only remarked lightly, 'Not quite. We've mended a few broken winows.'

Nikki felt the embers of combat stirring within her.

'Unnecessary expense,' she muttered. 'They could have been left boarded up.'

He looked so surprised by her hard attitude that Nikki kept silent as they entered the factory and she saw that not only had it been swept clean inside, but that someone had ordered a major overhaul. The smell of new paint was unmistakable. How much had he spent?

She wished now that she hadn't had to leave the sanctuary of his house. There, all had been peace and harmony and she'd even been able to believe that she and Alexander could find love. Here, they were on different sides of the battle zone.

She felt a familiar surge of anger and frustration as she wondered what else the mice had been up to while the cat was safely tucked up in her sickbed, but she resolved to wait and find out exactly what the story was before she exploded.

She could tell by the thrumming vibrations that the machines were all running smoothly but there didn't seem to be anyone around. Finally they met a worker who told them that everyone was in the delivery bay.

'Come on,' said Alexander, looking concerned. He grabbed Nikki's hand and towed her after him. She let him. She was as worried as he was.

'Nice to see you back, Miss Marlow,' the man shouted after their departing backs.

Nikki got the overall impression that the delivery bay was bigger and cleaner than the last time she'd seen it, but it certainly wasn't any tidier. An incredible exploded bombsite of open boxes, bits of metal, invoice notes and packing straw was surrounded by a circle of wailing figures, lamenting as if a disaster of Biblical proportions had taken place.

She recognised Linda, Norman Thompson, Alan Marsh and a few others, but they were all behaving like lunatics, and she felt too confused to know what to say to them.

She was glad when Alexander strode into the middle of the scene and gripped Alan Marsh by the shoulders.

'Alan! What on earth's going on?'

Nikki felt shock, followed by embarrassment, as she saw that the engineer was crying. He'd taken off his black-rimmed glasses and the tears sprang from his eyes.

'It's the Italian hydraulics – they've made the connectors the wrong size.'

Alexander's face turned to stone as he registered the implications of this.

'Are you sure?' he asked.

Alan nodded his red head and spoke in ragged gulps. 'I've checked and rechecked. One of the measurements is out. The tubes won't slot in where they should. We're finished.'

Linda came forward and grasped his hand. 'Alan, we're not done for yet,' she told him earnestly.

'I told you – I've checked and rechecked. There's no way the undercarriages will fit on to the buggies. And we've not the time to send the connectors back to be adjusted.'

Alexander wouldn't accept this. 'Go over it once more, carefully,' he ordered. 'Explain it to me as you go and perhaps we'll come up with something.'

But Alan was right. The connectors were the wrong size to slide into the chrome barrels of the pram parts. The mechanisms the Italians had made were designed to provide a revolutionary new system of springing. Without the link, there was no way to show people how manoeuvrable the new buggies were.

'Perhaps we could show off the bodies of the prams,' suggested Nikki. 'They are very smart, and we could tell people how good the new mechanisms will be.'

She shivered in the silence that followed. She could hear her own words hanging forlornly in the loading bay's cold air like smoke. It would take more than promises to win over the all-important buyers.

'Have you checked every single widget or whatever they are?' she suggested. 'If we had even one that worked we could use it as a demonstrator.'

Alan's red head moved in a despondent

shake. 'I've checked them all.'

Nikki glanced at Alexander. He was silent, thoughtful and, she felt, not hopeful. Some of her old fury returned.

'What went wrong?' she demanded.

The engineer's shoulders moved in a shrug. 'All the stuff we order in from Europe comes in metric measurements. Most of our machinery uses imperial measurements. The conversion between the two couldn't have been accurate when we ordered the parts.'

Nikki looked again at Alexander. His eyes were full of calm resignation and she saw with baffled fury that he was preparing to concede defeat.

For a moment she wondered if he was right to give in, but all the steel that long years of fighting alone had built into her forced her to reject any such suggestion. It was all right for Alexander, he had another factory and a family home to sustain him. But Davidson's Baby Carriage Company was her very first field assignment, and she was personally responsible for recommending a rescue package. No way was she going to let it go down without a fight.

'Alan, do the parts have to be completely remade or could they be altered to fit?' she asked.

Alan was lost in his own world. It was Norman Thompson who answered her.

'They could be altered. Ay, they could that.'

'So call a courier. Get the stuff back to Italy,' said Nikki.

Linda looked at her and shook her head. 'I rang them already, love. You know that we jumped the queue in their order book. They're on to working on an order for the Italian Ministry of Defence now, and they say they wouldn't be allowed to stop. It's a matter of national security.'

'National humbug, more like,' snorted Nikki. 'Was the mistake theirs, by the way?'

'That's debatable,' answered Norman Thompson. 'Alan's blueprints are clearly marked as imperial, but they could argue that metric is standard these days.'

Nikki wouldn't give up; she *couldn't*. She shivered again as the cold from the stone floor seemed to strike up to her bones.

'Let's go where it's warm. Come through to the canteen. I'm going to keep going over this until I'm certain there's no alternative.'

Alexander's warm hand grasped her cold fingers. His eyes were astonished and proud. 'You're a fighter, I'll give you that, Nikki.'

She gave him a long, hard look. 'I'm a winner, too, and don't you forget it.'

She saw that he meant to support her. All traces of his earlier resignation had melted and he positively bristled with energy. The other men still seemed shell-shocked, but Alexander and Linda rallied round, helping Nikki to hand out hot coffees and cream cakes. Then she found and set up a whiteboard with lots of markers.

'Come on,' she urged. 'We don't give up until we've found a solution.'

She made suggestion after suggestion. She made reasonable suggestions and silly ones. She listened to technical stuff that made her head ache, but she wouldn't give up.

Finally Alan Marsh exploded. 'What's the use?' he cried bitterly. 'Your heart's in the right place, Nikki, but you don't know anything about engineering. I can't even explain to you properly what the problem is. We might as well all go home.'

Linda stood up and faced her fiancé. 'How far would me and Chloe have got if we'd given up so easily? Now tell us again, Alan, love. What's the problem, exactly?'

The engineer rubbed his tired eyes and put on his spectacles. Then he sat down again and once more went over the problem.

And suddenly, like a miracle, the technical members of the group came up with a way to alter the ends of the chrome parts so that the two necessary pieces could be attached to one another.

'It needs a special machine, though,' said Alan wearily. 'And even if we could find someone who's got one, they'd have to be able to turn out the job straight away.'

'I'll start ringing round,' said Linda.

Norman Thompson slapped his forehead. 'Wait! I know a fellow with one of those machines. He worked at a place that made guns for the army, but I'm going back a fair bit. When they put new machines in he took the old stuff home. It was a hobby with him, you know. Lathes, milling machines – lovely things they are, and all set up in his garden shed.'

Norman raced to the phone and Nikki ordered the parts repacked so that they'd be ready to move.

Inwardly, she didn't know how much faith she had in this old pal of Norman's. He could be dead by now and his machines melted down for scrap.

However, when Norman came back there was a smile on his face.

'Fred's willing! Ay, he says he'd love to do it. Let's get the stuff over there.'

Throughout the rest of that day and the

whole of the next, Alan and his team worked non-stop and by midnight of the second day the number of fixed prams and buggies had grown until they had a finished sample of each of the new models.

'Well done, everyone!' said Alexander. 'But I'm taking Nikki home now. This is only her second day at work, and she was supposed to be on light duties!'

The packing team looked really pleased with themselves.

'We'll have each pram wrapped and on the van ready to leave first thing in the morning,' they promised.

Even Alan Marsh looked calmer and happier at last.

'I'm going home for a bit of shut-eye, but I'll be here at first light.'

Nikki fell asleep on the front seat of Alexander's Jaguar on the way home. She was aware of him carrying her upstairs to her room.

'I'll see you in the morning,' he promised.

She was lost in black velvet before she could answer.

15

Darkness Before The Dawn

It was still dark when they arrived at the factory the next morning. Alexander yawned as he got out of his car. Nikki shivered in the early morning chill. She was aware of him watching her with concern in his eyes.

'You need a hot drink before we start,' he said firmly.

It was just like him to think of her before even checking how the packing had gone.

'I have to check the van first,' she told him, and headed at top speed for the delivery bay before Alexander could stop her.

She was delighted to see that the van was fully loaded and the driver was already there.

'Everything's in order, Miss Marlow,' he told her cheerfully. 'The load's been checked a hundred times.'

Nevertheless, Nikki counted the samples on the van and did a quick sweep of the loading bay, just to make sure that none of the precious buggies had been left behind.

Then she slipped over to her office. She hadn't had time yet to read the valuation report, but she meant to take it with her in case she got a chance to look at it during the fair.

Linda was already working at her desk.

'Good morning, Nikki. There's a heap of messages for you.'

'Allen Green!' exclaimed Nikki, looking at the first slip. 'What does he want?'

'To take you to dinner at the best restaurant in town,' said Linda, pointing to the message.

Nikki rapidly dialled her colleague's mobile number then threw the slip on top of Linda's desk.

'He'll have worked himself into some hole or other with one of my old clients,' Nikki prophesied to Linda while she waited for him to pick up. 'Well, he's mistaken if he thinks I'll drop everything to bail him out!'

She was right. Allen had been a bit too clever with the owner of a well-known racing stable, but Nikki spoke firmly over the man's bleating pleas for help.

'Sorry, Allen, but I've got to get ready for a crucial trade fair today.'

She cut the connection and Allen's squawks terminated abruptly.

A tingle of excitement ran through Nikki

as she visualised their new buggies on display at the Baby Carriage Show. The whole fate of the factory hung on today. There was no way she could think about anything else. Then she picked up the next message slip.

The single word 'mother' hit her like a bolt of lightning and she felt as if she had fallen off a high mountain.

She crumpled the pink paper in hands that were suddenly shaking and hurled the ball of paper across the room. Then she stood immobile, staring at her secretary with eyes that saw nothing until she realised that Linda was questioning her nervously.

'Nikki? Nikki, love? Is it bad news?'

'I don't know, Linda. But I think it probably is, yes.'

But the concern in the other girl's voice had touched Nikki's heart, and with the warm feeling came the answer to her dilemma. She knew where her priorities lay at last.

Her mind was made up, yet a soft breath of regret shook her whole body as she dialled the number of the nursing home from memory. A very young voice answered the phone breathlessly.

'Olwen speaking. Oh, Miss Marlow, is it you? I hope you didn't mind me phoning you, but Dr Evans is on leave today and, well, your mother's very poorly – do you see?'

'I see,' answered Nikki, in a mechanical whisper.

Behind her, she was aware of the door opening and Alexander walking in with a streaming mug in each hand. She heard him whispering with Linda, and then her secretary left the room. Nikki was glad. She needed Alexander now.

He joined her and started to rustle through the papers on the desk, looking for something. Olwen went on saying words Nikki didn't want to hear.

'Well, Miss Marlow. I know you're very busy but I beg you, you're needed here.'

Nikki nodded very slowly and her words came out in a long sigh. 'Yes, I know. I'm on my way.'

She put down the phone as if it was made of glass and turned to face Alexander. She needed him. She wanted the comfort she had learned he could give her.

She was so sure that he would support her that it was a dynamite surprise to be confronted by blazing tawny eyes.

'Are you out of your mind? This is no time to be running off to be with your old flame.'

The shock raced around her system like a physical blow.

Then she saw that he was holding the message slip from Allen Green.

Nikki was dazed, shaken, and underneath all that, angry. How dare he assume she would put her social life before the factory?

The hurt in her heart doubled, trebled, became more than she could bear. Unable to speak, she tried to push past him. His big body moved fast, and he blocked the doorway.

'Nikki, you're not going?'

She looked into his cold, angry eyes and refused to explain herself. This mistrustful and furious male was what her brain had been trying to warn her about. All men were unreliable. She'd been foolish to think she could throw away every lesson her mother's life had ever taught her about men.

She raised her head and spoke calmly. 'Let me pass, please.'

There was nothing in the furious eyes that met hers that encouraged her to soften or explain. She didn't know how he would react if he knew the true situation, and she didn't care. The fact that he was choosing to think the worst of her was all that mattered. He stared at her with eyes that told her she'd been judged and found wanting. Then he opened the door and bowed her through with exaggerated courtesy.

'Don't let me delay you from your so-important date at the best restaurant in town, Miss Marlow.'

Nikki fumed for most of the three-hour trip from Yorkshire to the Welsh coast nursing home, but as she got closer to the place where her mother lay dying, other thoughts took over.

The stones of the village looked light and clean and the coastal air smelled of salt.

Gulls cried overhead as she parked her car and then walked up the front steps to ring the bell of the home.

A young girl in a neat overall answered the door. When she realised who Nikki was, relief flooded over her plump shiny face.

'Oh, Miss Marlow! I'm so pleased you're here, and so will your mam be. She's rallied a bit, but I think she'll pass on tonight. Go with the tide, most likely. That's what they usually do.'

For all her youth, the pale green eyes that shone in the girl's homely face were kind and held a world of understanding.

'There's nothing to be frightened of, Miss Marlow. I thought I'd be scared out of my wits the first time I saw a patient slip away, but it's all very natural. And I'll be with you.'

Nicole Barton never did awake. There was no tearful mother and daughter reunion. Yet as Nikki perched on the edge of a bedside chair, listening to the ever-decreasing sighs and the gentle ebb of breath from the still figure in the bed, she was fiercely glad that she was there.

Olwen popped in and out throughout the long day bringing cups of tea, and when it was time for the doctor's rounds she insisted on sending Nikki out for a walk.

'Yes, Miss Marlow, off you go. You need the fresh air. Your mam will do nicely for ten minutes.'

Nikki paced along the cold sea front, feeling sad and aware of the natural world around her. The tide was full in, lapping at the stones on the beach, she noticed, and the January sky was huge over the grey line of the sea.

She stopped to watch the sun set in a starburst of yellow and silver-lined thunderclouds, feeling strangely peaceful as she inhaled the salt air and listened to the gulls.

The nursing home felt stuffy when she returned, but it was warm and she was learning to trust Olwen.

'What did you mean, about the tide?'

The Welsh woman cast her a sidelong

glance. 'It's on the ebb at three o'clock to-morrow morning.'

Nikki looked into the matter-of-fact green eyes. 'And you think my mother...?'

'There's no science to it, Dr Evans says.'

'And what else does he say?'

'That there's nothing else he can do for her now. But she's comfortable enough, poor thing.'

Nikki returned to her vigil on the hard chair. The hours seemed to pass very quickly and she felt a gentle stillness stealing into her soul as she kept watch over her mother.

She was very glad she had come.

She and Nicole had never been close, but she was the only mother Nikki would ever have, and she needed to make peace with how things had been, before she could move forward.

And now Nikki came to realise that for all her adult life she had been carrying around with her the anger of a child for the mother who hadn't been perfect. As the anger drained away, she was able to remember the good times as well. A few laughs, a pretty dress, a night cuddled up in bed scoffing deliciously hot fish and chips under the blankets.

Nikki was old enough now to appreciate that her mother had never left her, or passed her on to the care of the state. She'd been fed, she'd been housed, and if life hadn't been perfect, Nikki could appreciate the fact that Nicole had always shared what she had with her.

'You did your best for me,' she admitted aloud.

She reached out and lightly touched the thin hand that lay on top of the sheet. Nikki had always striven so hard for money and independence, but all along what she had really wanted was exactly the same things her mother had been scrambling after – love and a family.

Nikki remembered how her poor mother had hated to be alone, and wrapped her fingers gently around the fragile bones of Nicole's hand. It was impossible to tell whether her mother knew she was there or not, but she was still holding her hand when Nicole Barton finally slipped away.

Following blind instinct, Nikki walked out of the nursing home and into the night, or rather, the early morning. The cold chilled her tears on her face, but she was glad to be out in the fresh air.

The long line of pewter-grey water was far enough down the beach for Nikki to see that Olwen had been right about her mother going out with the tide. Life and death. Ebb and flow. She stood looking over the hushed dark beach for a while, soaking up the calm whispering of the lapping waves.

A single bright star hung under a slice of silver moon, lighting up the quiet sky. Alexander would know what the star was called. She wished she could ask him about it.

The pre-dawn cold was making her shiver. She walked over to her car and rummaged in the boot with cold hands. She found an extra sweater and wrapped a scarf around her neck.

Then she stepped lightly on to the hard-packed sand and set off towards the craggy line of cliffs at the other end of the bay, walking quite fast, feeling the turmoil in her heart settle as she said goodbye to her painful past and found a new peace filling her heart.

Nikki felt calm by the time she reached the curving tip of the bay. She turned and looked back towards where she had come from. On the east side of the bay, the sky was glowing brightly and a brilliant streak of gold lit the horizon. The gleaming wet sand was empty save for a flock of tiny birds that ran piping along the water's edge, and a tall dark figure, moving purposefully towards her.

She didn't need the supernatural tingle

deep in her bones to tell her it was Alexander. She felt a smile lifting her lips as she walked to meet him. How silly and trivial their row seemed now. The last remnants of her old suspicion crumbled into smoke and blew away in the fresh sea air. Of course she could trust him. He had been an idiot, but wasn't everyone now and then? And the expression on his face as he came to a hesitant stop before her told her that he was feeling the utter depths of remorse.

His eyes held a world of regret.

'Nikki, I'm so sorry.' His deep voice was tentative.

She looked steadily into his brown eyes and tried to make it easy for him.

'I should have explained. It was my fault.'

The light that sprang to life in his eyes was brighter than any dawn as he realised that she was going to give him a chance.

'I didn't give you time to explain. Oh, Nikki, what a crass, bumbling, total blockhead I am.'

His eyes searched her face. The light grew stronger about them and the gulls whirled overhead, greeting the new morning with bright, wild cries. Alexander looked oddly humble.

'I've never been jealous before,' he told

her. 'It turned me into a monster. I'm ashamed of myself.'

He took his hands out of his pockets and made as if he would reach for her, but then his hands fell back by his sides.

'Can you ever forgive me?'

She met the honest repentance in his brown eyes. Of course she forgave him, but she couldn't resist prolonging the moment just a little longer.

'How did you find out where I was?'

'Linda. I growled and grouched the whole day through. Everyone else was avoiding me, but she had the nerve to find out what the matter was, and she put me right about a few things.'

Nikki's heart warmed.

'So you came straight here to find me?'

He nodded.

She could resist no longer. She reached out and touched his hand.

'I'm glad you came.'

He grasped her hand eagerly and held it as if it were precious. His brown eyes hunted for the truth in her eyes.

'Truly?'

'I missed you,' she confessed frankly. 'I missed your support.'

Anguish twisted his expression.

'The exhibition I made of myself earlier wasn't very supportive,' he said.

'Everyone makes mistakes,' she told him, feeling the peace that the words gave her in her heart. 'We're all human. All we can do is love each other and do our best.'

Alexander's arms reached out for her now, and he drew her against the warmth of his strong chest, where she had so longed to be. As she moved close into the softness of his fleecy sweater, Nikki felt whole at last, and she knew that her love for this man would never make her a slave or weigh her down.

'I'm not afraid to love you any more,' she told him.

In the silence that followed she felt the strong, steady beat of his heart.

'You never told me your mother was so ill.'

A few tears welled and clung to Nikki's lashes.

'She had a series of strokes after her last husband left her.'

Alexander touched her cheekbone lightly with a finger.

'There are shadows under your eyes, Nikki. You must be bone weary. Let me take you home.'

She rested her head against his chest.

'I am home,' she told him, soaking up his

warmth and his strength and his caring. 'I never want to go anywhere without you again.'

'You shan't,' he told her, and his lips claimed hers in a promise.

He broke the delicious kiss too soon for Nikki's liking.

'Later!' he told her, with a butterfly kiss on her forehead, her chin and both cheeks. 'I'm going to devote the rest of my life to making you happy.' He looked anxiously at her and added, 'If you'll let me.'

Nikki laughed delightedly. 'Is that ring still in your pocket?' she asked.

'I thought it would be unlucky to carry it around. After the way I treated you, I never dreamed you'd say yes.'

She couldn't help hugging him again.

'When we get back, then, I'll be proud to wear your ring.'

He looked so happy as he took her hand and they walked together along the beach. Fresh sea air blew all around them and Nikki could taste salt on her lips. The sky was lightening to a fine pale blue, and a few crisp clouds streaked the horizon. The far-away circle of a January sun was rising in the sky, turning the waves to cream-tipped cobalt.

Nikki was content to walk without talking.

Alexander's warm fingers twined around hers seemed to infuse her with warmth and new energy.

When they got back to the nursing home she turned to him. 'I don't see your car,' she commented, puzzled.

A slightly embarrassed flush stained his cheeks. 'I hired one. And a plane.'

Her mouth dropped open. 'You did what?'

His eyes held a trace of remembered agony. 'I needed to find you. You were all alone, and I'd been such a fool.'

She went into his arms.

'I'm not alone now.'

'Never again,' he promised her.

And he kept his promise, staying by her side, helping her to take care of the arrangements following her mother's death.

'Shall I book you into a hotel until after the funeral?' he asked her.

Nikki felt a shock like a river in flood run over her.

'The fair! It's the Harrogate Fair today! Alexander, we must go!'

She could see by the light in his eyes how much he wanted to go, but he still held back.

'Are you sure?'

'Are you driving to the airport? Or am I?'

Alexander wanted to kiss her all the way to Harrogate. She kept trying to protest. 'I've never been in a little plane before. Let me look out of the window.'

But her long night had left her exhausted and she slipped into a delicious light doze, only waking when they disembarked at the tiny airstrip near Harrogate.

'You should go straight to a hotel,' Alexander told her in the taxi on their way to the exhibition hall. 'This is madness. You've had no sleep at all.'

She pushed aside the exhaustion that surrounded her. 'I don't need sleep,' she said firmly.

His brown eyes were so dark and loving as he said, 'But I need to take good care of you, Nikki.'

'Then get me to our exhibition stand or I'll go mad.'

He gave in at that, recognising the truth in her comment. Hand in hand they raced up the steps that led to the purpose-built hall.

The exhibition space was as busy as a city railway station and Nikki paused, feeling the noise and confusion wash over her.

'Where's our stand?'

'Over here.'

She clutched Alexander's hand and her

eyes swept the hall.

'How's it going? How's it going?' she chattered impatiently.

His look was full of amusement. 'I don't know. I've been in Wales with you, remember?'

Holding hands they approached the stand. It was strange to see the familiar prams and buggies displayed on plinths under spotlights. Nikki's anxious eyes swept over the stylish new designs, the sporting new colours, the beautifully printed pillows, and she felt herself relax a little.

'They look good!' she said confidently.

Alexander's calm surface was cracking just a little.

'Oh, they're good, all right. But is anyone buying them?'

Now they were close enough to see that all the staff were standing motionless around the display, looking uncomfortable.

Nikki felt faint. 'It would appear not,' she muttered.

'All the buyers spent ages looking,' explained Linda unhappily when they questioned her, 'but they've moved on without placing any orders.'

Nikki stood watching the crowds go by. She realised that she and Alexander had joined the motionless tableau presented by the other staff, but she could think of nothing to do, no action that would save them.

Then Norman Thompson stiffened and quivered like a greyhound at the starting gate.

'Hey up! That buyer's from a supermarket chain – and it looks like he's coming back to us.'

The frozen group watched a middle-aged man in a blue suit head in their direction. Every eye was trained on him in mesmerised, hopeful silence, while Nikki's heart was thumping so uncomfortably that she thought she was going to be sick. And if he walked straight past them, she knew she was going to collapse on the spot.

However, he stopped at their stand and stood looking about him, smiling amiably at the new buggies. Nikki couldn't move. Go on, someone, she thought frantically, talk to him before he changes his mind and walks away. But nobody stirred. It was left to Norman Thompson to make a move.

'Now then, Ted. Have you come to give us an order?'

The silence that followed was cruel, but finally the buyer spoke.

'I have that. I think they'll sell well, these

new designs of yours. I'm going to put the full range in all our stores. I like them a lot.'

The relief was so great that Nikki would have fallen over if Alexander hadn't been keeping a tight hold on her. Of course the buyers would have wanted to check on what the other stands were offering before placing any orders. No wonder the stand had been quiet at first.

As if to prove her theory, a curly-haired woman in a red coat walked straight up to the stand.

'I've been right around now and my mind's made up,' she said, pointing at one of Alan's most radical designs. 'I want the Cowes buggy, the Wimbledon pram and that amazing cross-country three-wheeler. I've got a small shop so I'll only be taking samples, but I'll have a pile of brochures as well, please. I'm sure my customers will want more.'

Brochures! thought Nikki frantically. She wanted to kick herself for not having produced such an important sales tool.

Then Linda stepped forward and spoke to the woman.

'Let me have your address and I'll post you the proper brochure when it arrives from the printers. Meantime, would you like some of these sheets?'

The customer took the sheets of glossy paper rather disdainfully at first, but as she noted the clear colour photographs with the full technical specifications listed neatly underneath, she relaxed.

'These are fine. Can I have one hundred for each model, please?'

Linda looked rather startled, but answered calmly enough: 'Of course. I'll have them for you in a moment.'

Nikki followed her secretary over to the order table where a colour printer was plugged into a laptop.

'Linda, you're wonderful! But when did you find time to do these?'

'I got my cousin out of bed at three this morning and borrowed his camera. Then we stayed up for hours, putting it all together.'

Nikki saw now that the attractive background of the photographs wasn't the sporting horse stable it appeared to be, but a cunningly chosen corner of the factory loading bay. She couldn't help gurgling with laughter.

'Straw from the packing crates, and isn't that Norman's tartan-lined coat? I can't believe how glamorous you've made it all look.'

Linda flushed and looked pleased.

'Oh, Linda, they're brilliant!' said Nikki fervently.

One buyer after another approached the stand. Some placed big orders. More, like the first woman, ordered a few samples and asked for a brochure.

Nikki went to Alexander and took his hand, feeling pure delight as she realised she had the right to walk up to him and kiss his cheek any time she chose.

'We need more paper for the printer,' she told him. 'I'm going to slip out and get some.'

He looked down at her and smiled. 'Oh no, you're not,' he said. 'You're exhausted. You're going to book into a hotel, young lady.'

Nikki could feel how weary her bones were now, but it was worth it to experience the sweetness of being looked after.

He drew her close, as if he were tucking her under the shelter of his wing. Then he waved a hand at the busy staff and the crowd of buyers.

'You can relax now, Nikki. Let others do their part.'

As he bent his head and took his time about kissing her, Nikki melted into his arms and felt no desire to hurry him. Deep in her heart she let go of the last of the heavy burdens she had been carrying, and trusted in life and love at last.

This Large Print Book, for people
who cannot read normal print,
is published under the auspices of

THE ULVERSCROFT FOUNDATION